The Takeover Effect

Also by Nisha Sharma

Young Adult Fiction
MY SO-CALLED BOLLYWOOD LIFE

The Takeover Effect

THE SINGH FAMILY TRILOGY

NISHA SHARMA

AVONIMPULSE
An Imprint of HarperCollinsPublishers

THE TAKEOVER EFFECT. Copyright © 2019 by Nisha Seesan. All rights reserved. Printed in the United States of America. No part of this book may be used or reproduced in any manner whatsoever without written permission except in the case of brief quotations embodied in critical articles and reviews. For information, address HarperCollins Publishers, 195 Broadway, New York, NY 10007.

Digital Edition APRIL 2019 ISBN: 978-0-06-285417-9
Print Edition ISBN: 978-0-06-285437-7

Cover design by Nadine Badalaty
Cover photograph © Lorado/iStock/Getty Images

Avon Impulse and the Avon Impulse logo are registered trademarks of HarperCollins Publishers in the United States of America.

Avon and HarperCollins are registered trademarks of HarperCollins Publishers in the United States of America and other countries.

FIRST EDITION

19 20 21 22 23 HDC 10 9 8 7 6 5 4 3 2 1

To my husband. It took you long enough to find me.

Acknowledgments

A BOOK IS a team effort, and *The Takeover Effect* would've never happened without the amazing support of a few very important people in my life. First, thanks to my agent, Joy Tutela, at David Black Literary for always being open to my zany new ideas. Joy, without your support, half of the books I write wouldn't have happened. To Elle Keck for remaining calm and collected whenever I was on the verge of losing my cool. Elle, thank you for always believing in me. To Caridad Pineiro, author, mentor, and confidant. Your legal expertise was fantastic, and any and all errors in this book are completely my fault. And to my friends Smita Kurrumchand and Ali Magnotti-Nagel, for reading early copies and telling me my writing was good even though I know it wasn't. Your support keeps me going, guys. Next round is on me.

The Takeover Effect

Prologue

DEEPAK SINGH WAS the fifth son of a fifth son. He was born in a village on the outskirts of Chandigarh, Punjab, India, and was fortunate enough to receive a boarding school education. His father was a police officer, as were his brothers, but Deepak wanted something different. He wanted something more. In his heart of hearts, he wasn't a warrior like his brothers or the ancestors that came before him. He was a poet, and his poetry was code.

Deepak knew his obsession with code was sometimes difficult to communicate, which was why he needed his morning walks to clear his head and work on his messaging. He approached the carved wooden bench that overlooked the front gardens on his estate and took a seat. The sky was a blend of orange and deep blue already, and he settled down to watch the remainder of the sunrise. A gentle spring breeze cooled his weathered skin, and he let out a sigh. He needed to ask his wife to join him on his walks again so she could enjoy the scenery with him.

He took out the faded sepia picture of his family that he carried in his billfold and looked at the unmarred face of his youth. He remembered the two heavy red leather suitcases he carried, and the determined look on his wife's face as they exited customs at John F. Kennedy International Airport for the first time all those years ago. He'd come to America to pursue his dreams, and in thirty years, Deepak had started the company Bharat, Inc., become a leading subject matter expert in image processing using deep learning, registered fifteen patents related to image recognition, and amassed a small fortune. He continued to live his life with Guru Nanak's teachings in mind and raised his three strong sons the same way.

His sons. His joy. They also lived life with Guru Nanak's teachings and wore their commitment to god in the form of a silver kara he'd given each of them as they entered manhood.

His youngest, Zail, was the most like him, and therefore the easiest for him to understand. They spent hours together in their tech lab situated in Silicon Valley. Zail wore his bracelet in silence and devotion.

His middle son wore his kara and his commitment to family like a badge of honor. Ajay was in line for CEO and he was a powerful leader. Deepak just wished he lived for more than just the business. Like Hem used to.

Hem. Hemdeep. His firstborn and the most complicated of all of his boys. Deepak rubbed the heel of his hand against his chest as a spike of pain shot through his heart. He'd always thought Hem would lead his empire when he was gone, but after their . . . disagreement, Hem refused to participate in the family business anymore. Deepak knew he was a part of the reason why Hem left, and even though he'd seen Hem over the last year and a half, their relationship was strained. All he wanted was his son's happiness. If he couldn't ensure that, then all of his money was worthless.

The pain returned in his chest, following a slight tingle. Carefully putting his picture away, he stood on shaking legs and began the slow trek back to the house. Hem would have to find his own away in business and in love. Deepak just hoped that his son wouldn't lose sight of family in the process.

Chapter One

IN SEVENTY-TWO HOURS, Hemdeep Singh had flown halfway around the world, led seven meetings for his client, reviewed hundreds of OSHA guidance documents, and taken a tour of two plants and warehouse facilities. The final contract negotiations were underway, and if he could secure the multimillion-dollar agreement, he'd have another successful win for his new firm.

The hotel he used as his home base for negotiations in the Philippines was a hotbed for tycoons and wealthy families because it provided discretion and luxury. Next to the bar that snaked along one side of the waterfall, where bartenders decorated drinks with exotic flowers, Hem swirled the top-shelf whiskey in his tumbler before toasting Faisal Rao, a magnate in the renewable energy industry. Faisal was also a vicious negotiator and had graduated from a top ten law school before investing his family's fortune in enterprise.

"Section 27.8 won't affect your bottom line, but it'll protect both my client and you from tax concerns."

Faisal hummed and scratched his beard. "I'm likely to agree with you—"

"Then we can sign."

"*But* I want my team to take a look at it."

Damn it, Hem thought. There wasn't a chance in hell of wrapping up the agreement within the hour if Faisal sent it back to his team. They were slow as shit.

"You know your business better than they do," Hem countered. "It's you that's taking the risk."

Faisal grinned. "That's very true." He leaned back in his seat and crossed his arms over his thick chest. "That's why I'm thinking my team should review it. I don't want to make any rushed decisions since I'll be paying the penalty."

"We can go back and forth like this forever," Hem said.

Faisal let out a laugh. "You're right. And on that note, it's nice to see another Indian from the States entrenched in global contract negotiation. We're a rarity, and our conversations have been a pleasure. Are you a Singh from Rajasthan or Singh from—?"

"Punjab. Sikh Punjabi from Chandigarh. My relatives still live there." Hem hated this type of small talk but if he could connect with Faisal on a personal level, then he'd bare his soul like he was talking to a shrink just to close the deal.

"My father's family came from Chandigarh originally," the man said with apparent joy. "My father was desperate to wear a turban and carry a sword in his youth like the traditional Sikh men he saw growing up. So he's said. Honestly, your height should've clued me in. What are you, six-two?"

"Six-four."

"Yes, your height is definitely a trademark quality of a Sikh man. You know, I was surprised that Tevish was using such a young firm to handle the negotiation. It couldn't have just been your height and looks that landed his account."

Pride.

Faisal was dragging his feet because his pride was injured. Hem relaxed in his seat and grinned at his opponent. Here he was, CEO of a successful midsize business, having to work with an outside law firm on a negotiation. Hem could understand executives that were level-conscious. He'd been the same way when he first started working with his father. It had taken him some time to learn that Deepak Singh didn't care what position a person held in his company. They were all treated with respect. That didn't mean executives outside Bharat agreed with the same philosophy, though.

"Tevish's family has deep connections with mine. I worked as an executive for my family business for years after law school so he knew that I could handle something as important as your agreement."

"Oh? What's your family business?"

"Bharat, Inc."

Faisal's eyes nearly bugged out of his head. "Your father is . . ."

"Deepak Singh, yes."

"Why aren't you still working for the company?"

"Because my father's business is growing and I need to expand my experience to help it along. Having the right industry knowledge is important in the technology space."

He'd repeated those words so many times and they felt stale on his tongue. Very few people knew of the heartache, the pain that had triggered his decision to leave. His parents and their involvement in his life were part of the reason why he'd lost his fiancée. Working closely with them was too difficult after he'd gotten his heart obliterated. On top of that, he needed to follow his passion. He'd only ever known Bharat, and it felt too unstructured, too relaxed for him. He wanted more, needed more, and starting his own law firm and investment group had been the best thing he'd ever done.

"Come on, Faisal," Hem said when he was met with silence. "You can't be scared of me now that you know my history."

Faisal's fingers fluttered over the edges of the tablet he'd been referencing. "I'm scared of nobody, kid.

I've been at this for a lot longer than you. Honestly, I simply wanted to know how you got so damn good at bullshitting. Now I know. It makes sense why Tevish sent you now."

Hem grinned. He was closing in on the win. He could feel it. "You should've never doubted him."

Hem felt his phone buzz in his pocket and he discreetly reached inside his jacket and silenced the device. "Sign the contract. You'll make a shit ton of money if you do."

"I'm beginning to warm to the idea. Only because I have a feeling you'll never stop bugging me until I do."

Hem's phone began to buzz again.

"Do you need to get that?"

The phone stopped. "No, I—" When it started buzzing again, he took it out and read his brother's name on the screen. "Yeah, actually, give me a second." He didn't spare Faisal another look as he stood from the small table they'd occupied and walked a few feet away for some privacy.

"Ajay, what is it?"

His brother's gruff voice answered immediately. "I'm calling in the troops, brother."

"I'll be back in New York in two days."

"No, you have to come home now."

Hem snorted. "Home? Like the estate? It's better if I keep my distance for a little while longer. Dad still shits himself every time I'm around."

"I'm not fucking around, Hem."

Something in Ajay's voice drained Hem's humor. "What's wrong?"

"Have you checked your email yet?"

"No, was I supposed to?"

"Do it."

Hem opened up his email and saw a message forwarded from his brother. The original message came from Hans Fineburg, CEO of WTA Digital.

TO THE CEO AND CHAIRMAN OF THE BOARD, BOARD OF DIRECTORS, AND LEADERSHIP COUNCIL OF BHARAT, INC.

This missive, adherent to SEC guidelines, constitutes a formal offer of purchase . . .

"What the fuck is this?" Hem snapped.

"That's not all of it," Ajay said. "Dad had a heart attack after the letter hit our inboxes this morning."

Hem felt as if Ajay had sucked all the air out of his lungs. "Is Dad . . . Is he okay?"

"He's in the hospital, but stable. We haven't told any of the extended family or staff yet. We're keeping it quiet. How soon can you be stateside?"

Hem didn't see eye to eye with his father, but they were still family, and he would do anything for family. He checked his Rolex. "It'll take me at least a day. I'm in fucking Manila, Ajay. It's not like they have hourly flights to the US."

"Didn't you take your jet?"

"No, I sold it to pay for overhead costs on my firm."

"Damned inconvenient, Hem."

"I didn't want to dip into my earnings from Bharat or my trust to raise the money."

"It's still inconvenient. I'll check with a supplier to see if we can borrow one of their jets for now. If not, I don't know, chopper to the next largest international airport and book a private jet from there. There is a board meeting in less than twenty-four hours."

"Did Dad make that decision?"

"No, the fucking board chatted with each other like a bunch of aunties and decided to establish a compensation committee immediately to address the offer. They're restless since we haven't met sales targets after we went public. We've got to get them in line before they try to oust Dad."

Ajay was born to be a leader. He'd done amazing work since Hem had left the business and had shark like instincts. If he was worried, things had to be in bad shape. "I'll be there for the meeting. Whatever you need. How's Mom holding up?"

There was a deep, frustrated sigh on the other end of the phone. "How do you think? She's a goddamn rock, man. Yelled at Dad the moment she saw him in the hospital room. Said that he got what he deserved for eating too much mango pickle at night. As if that's the cause of a heart attack."

Hem missed his mother, sometimes painfully. Her

predictable reaction made him smile. "Thank god for small blessings. I'm going to get myself to the airport. Let me know what you can do."

"Got it. See you soon, brother."

Hem hung up and walked back over to Faisal who was reading the last set of provisions on his tablet again.

"Everything okay?" he said.

"No. Sorry, but I need to go."

Faisal flipped the cover over his tablet and straightened in his seat. "No problem. This will give me time to review with my team again—"

"No." Hem picked up the tablet which was luckily still unlocked. He scrolled to the bottom of the page, pulled out a stylus, and held it out. "I know you don't want to give up control over this financial aspect, but fuck it, Faisal. You're going to be rich. Stop stalling."

Faisal gave him an even look but he took the stylus and quickly scribbled his name.

Hem did the same for his portion, and they signed six more sections before Hem saved the document and passed the tablet back to Faisal so he could send it through to Hem's email.

"Happy now?" Faisal said.

"Thrilled. It's been a pleasure doing business." Hem picked up his drink and drained the last of its contents before grabbing his coat and his briefcase. He hated himself for wasting those precious five minutes on this guy when all he wanted to do was get home to his father, but he wouldn't get this opportunity again.

As he rode up to his floor, he thought about his father and the bitter words they exchanged the last time they spoke. After Deepak Singh meddled in his life so coldly, so painfully, they had never seemed to see eye to eye again.

This takeover attempt and a heart attack changed everything. He still loved his father and despite everything that had happened, he'd do anything to help salvage Bharat, even if it meant coming back to the company.

Hem keyed into his room and booted up his laptop to draft a quick message to his paralegals, his assistant, and the ten attorneys that worked for him.

I know we're just getting our feet wet, but I need you to divide and take my case load temporarily. I'll sign all the necessary paperwork to transition it to you, but I'll be out of the office for the next few weeks. You can still reach me by email and my cell if it's an emergency.

He gave detailed follow-up instructions to his paralegal and his assistant and then began to pack all of his items in his small carry-on bag.

Dread filled his gut at the thought of letting go of the reins on a business that had been his salvation after Bharat. Hopefully his father could see, after the time that had passed, that he'd made the right choice.

But now wasn't the time to think about old arguments and family politics. His father needed him, his brothers needed him, and there was nothing Hem wouldn't do to protect them.

"The eldest Singh has returned like a Bollywood fucking hero," Hem mused to himself as he zipped up his bag.

Chapter Two

Mina Kohli lay sleepless in bed like she did every year on this day. The muted sounds of an early New York City morning filtered through the open window as a backdrop to the drifting memories of her mother. Mina couldn't help but wonder what kind of relationship they'd have if she was still alive. It'd been fifteen years since the accident, but that didn't matter. Every birthday reminded her of the hole in her heart and in her life.

A familiar ping echoed through the bedroom and Mina reached out to pick up her phone.

DAD: You'll get through today.

Simple, short, and to the point. Her father wasn't an affectionate man, nor were he and Mina close, but sometimes he managed to say just the right thing at the right moment. She sent back a response.

> MINA: Just like I always do. Hopefully I'll see you at the office.
> DAD: No. Working from home. I'll ask my assistant to schedule a lunch later this week.
> MINA: Okay, Dad.
> DAD: Okay. Happy thirtieth birthday, Mina.

"That's as close to a touching father-daughter moment as we've ever had," Mina muttered. With a sigh, she opened up her photos and clicked through the albums until she found the one labeled 'Mom'.

Pictures filled the screen. Her mother looked like her. Long dark hair, eyes too big for her face, and sharp cheekbones. Mina scrolled through the pregnancy photos, the baby photos, and the pictures of the few times they went to Central Park when she was a child.

Shalini Kaur Kohli had been such a powerhouse her entire short life, with an active career and social life. No matter what, she'd always made time for Mina. She'd been a mother, a wife, a litigator, and a sister who raised two younger brothers to be litigators as well. Her life had ended the day her brothers voted her out of the firm she built from the ground up. She'd gotten raging drunk, then climbed behind the wheel of her sedan. Mina discovered the truth about the accident when she was seventeen. That's when she began her mission to take back her birthright. Nothing was going to stop her.

Except maybe an arranged marriage.

She shifted against her silk pillowcase, thinking about her uncle's offer. If she married Virat, the son of the managing partner at J.J.S. Immigration Law, she'd get the equity partner position at her mother's firm. Her marriage would make way for the union of two of the largest South Asian-owned firms in the country.

The problem was that she wasn't attracted to Virat. He was such a nice guy, but unfortunately, he possessed the personality of a cardboard box.

Mina's phone buzzed in her hand. Her eyebrows rose clear to her hairline when she saw Sanjeev's number. Her uncle rarely called her, and never at four in the morning. Maybe he remembered it was her birthday. Doubtful, but Sanjeev was full of surprises.

"Yes?"

"You agree to the partner position yet, girl?"

Mina slowly sat up. "No, I'm still thinking it through."

"What the hell is taking you so long?"

"You're basically bartering me for an immigration firm. I deserve some time."

His gruff voice boomed in her ear. "There may be another way to get you that equity partner position. Get to the office. There is an emergency board meeting at

Bharat, Inc., and you're the only senior associate with patent experience who has the bandwidth to take on another case. If you're here in an hour, that'll give you, oh, three hours to prep on the company, the other board members, and WTA Digital."

Mina's mind raced as she tried to piece together facts. Bharat had recently gone public, but they were floundering, or so the news said. Sanjeev was friendly with the CEO and chairman, which was how he'd been selected to be part of the board. WTA Digital, however . . . Well, their name was as well-known as Google. A tech company that was in bed with the government. They did everything from artificial intelligence and smartphones, to government defense projects and NATO commissioned research.

"Mina! Are you there?"

"I'm here. Let me guess. Offer for purchase?"

"Just get to the office, girl."

Even though Mina hated her uncle, his words made her smile. Once she'd put in her dues, she'd slowly edge out her uncles. Then she'd take the firm to another level, one that would make her mother proud. Cases like a WTA takeover would be the norm for her.

As she showered, she dictated to her digital assistant and drafted emails to her legal assistant and paralegal. She needed to rearrange her schedule, which meant shifting two client calls and asking for an extra day to review a contract.

Mina slipped into a maroon suit dress with matching pumps and a coordinating Chanel bag. Because it took her an extra minute to pile her long hair on top of her head in a sleek updo, she had to call for a car to pick her up in front of her apartment building in Chelsea.

"Looking lovely today, Ms. Kohli," George said as he opened the door for her. "Spring weather at its finest."

"Thanks, George. I may have a meeting with a new client today."

"Knock 'em dead."

"I always do."

The car was already waiting at the curb, and in a practiced move, she folded herself into the back seat and answered emails for the entire drive to Park and 40th.

The lights were on in the building when she scanned her badge and stepped through the glass doors and into the offices for Kohli and Associates. She loved the rows of redwells stacked on top of the filing cabinets that hardly anyone used anymore, the desks for the paralegals and assistances crammed with paper, discarded coffee cups, and personal items. Most of all, she loved that her floor was high enough to get a view of the East River along one row of windows. Sometimes when she was going for a run or binging on movies at her condo, she'd imagine this exact view was spread out in front of her.

"Mina?" her uncle roared from his corner office.

She headed toward the sound, passing empty cubicles

THE TAKEOVER EFFECT 19

along the way. When she reached her uncle's assistant's desk, she paused to admire the woman typing away at the keyboard. Except for the circles under her eyes, Sangeeta was pressed and polished, as if it wasn't five thirty in the morning.

"Good morning, Mina. He's ready for you."

"Why don't you get some coffee, Sangeeta?"

"No, I'm okay."

Mina pulled out her company card and handed it to her. "Get something for yourself. Pastry, too. And if you don't mind, coffees for me and the dragon."

She glanced at his office and then back to Mina. "I shouldn't . . ."

"I'll keep him busy. You look like you could use some fresh air. I think the cart downstairs just opened up."

Sangeeta glanced one more time at Sanjeev's open door before she quickly grabbed her small purse from a bottom drawer in her desk. "Thanks, Mina."

"Anytime. You can always come to me if you need anything. I know that you trusted my mom when you worked for her. I want you to know that you can trust me, too."

"I—I'll be right back," she said before she scrambled down the hall.

"Mina!" her uncle roared again.

She stepped into the corner office, ignoring the smell of stale cigarettes. The space was a pigsty with papers everywhere. There were discarded suitcoats and ties, dirty bowls and mugs, and an overflowing ashtray. She passed the small conference table and dropped her bag into one of his client chairs.

Her uncle turned in his high-back chair, dressed in a black suit and wearing a thunderous scowl. "What took you so long?"

"You said an hour."

"Whatever. Sit down."

Mina pulled her tablet out of her bag and sat in the second chair. "WTA Digital wants to purchase Bharat. The board is going to have to appoint a committee to determine if the value of the offer is equivalent to the value of the company based on forecasting and financials. Depending on the technicality of the patents Bharat has and how well management at Bharat cooperates, it'll take a while to make that decision. This whole thing could take anywhere from ten days to months. WTA's offer is only good for thirty days, but that can be renegotiated."

Her uncle leaned back in his chair, resting his hands on his round belly. "Good. That's very good. I want you to head the committee that's reviewing the offer."

"The committee has to be an impartial party."

Sanjeev ran two fingers over his mustache. "I talked to a friend of mine who handles high profile acquisition cases. Even though I'm on the board, it wouldn't be a conflict of interest if one of my attorneys takes the case. As long as they don't report to me. I also talked to Deepak's son at Bharat. They're okay with my firm's involvement. The remaining members of the committee will be se-

THE TAKEOVER EFFECT 21

lected by the rest of the board. They'll need to be experts in business intelligence, integrity, and finance."

"Okay. You do realize that I'll have to be on site a couple times a week, right? I do have the bandwidth to take this on since I just closed out a bunch of cases, but court dates, depositions, and meetings for the rest of my workload will have to be rescheduled."

"Fine. Do what you have to do. I want the committee to make a decision as quickly as possible, so if that means you set up a makeshift office there, so be it. Oh, and there is one more thing."

"Shoot."

"I'll make you equity partner, with or without the arranged marriage to Virat, if you report to the Bharat board at the end of your review that we need to take WTA's offer."

Mina jerked in her seat. "What the hell?" She couldn't have heard him right. There was no way he'd just asked her point-blank to commit a crime.

"I know you don't want to marry Virat," Sanjeev continued. "I also know you'll do whatever it takes to become partner. I'm willing to give you another opportunity. One that doesn't include an arranged marriage. Make the WTA deal happen, Mina. If you can't, then it's wedding bells for you. Unless of course, you'd rather be unemployed."

Sanjeev looked too smug, too content. Was he testing her, or trying to get rid of her? She'd do anything to get her mother's company back, except lose her integrity.

"I feel like I'm in an alternate universe. Sanjeev, you aren't seriously asking me to sabotage the vote."

"This is how the real world works, Mina. I shouldn't have to explain myself. Bharat is in the process of registering a patent for software that can locate moving targets traveling over two hundred miles an hour with ninety-eight point eight seven percent accuracy. It's my friend's latest invention in an effort to find missing persons across the world. However, I'm a lawyer and a businessman. I know that they'll never be able to do it. WTA has the resources and manpower to successfully execute the research."

"How the hell did you find this out?"

"Oh, the R&D team presented to the board last quarter," Sanjeev said, waving his hand in dismissal. "Just look like you're doing a due diligence review, but in the end, your report should have one conclusion. It's not only for your future's sake, but also because it's the smartest move."

Sanjeev wasn't telling her the whole truth. That much was clear. He was asking Mina to jeopardize her license and do something unethical for the sake of staying at the firm. Did she appear so driven that he assumed she'd consider risking her future for a chance at a partner position?

Mina should've thrown his proposition back in his face, when something about his expression made her pause.

Bingo.

If she pretended to go through with his plan, it would buy her time to find out if her uncle had waded into anything illegal himself.

She stood and picked up her bag. "Fine. I'll consider . . . all of this. When do we leave for the board meeting?"

"Two hours. Remember, I'm counting on you to make the right decision for both your career and this law firm. It's about time I get some use out of you."

Her hand tightened on her purse handle. "I'll be in my office."

She left the stifling room, her brain running through legal ethics violations and consequences that Sanjeev could be involved in when she ran straight into Sangeeta.

"Uh, Ms. Kohli? Your coffee and card."

"Oh. Thanks, Sangeeta."

Sangeeta picked up a small wrapped package from her desk and held it out. "And I got you this," she said quietly. "I was reviewing your employment contract for signature and saw your birth date. I know you haven't celebrated it in a while, and a croissant isn't much compared to a cake but . . ."

"No, it's okay. You don't have to—"

"Happy thirtieth birthday."

"Oh. Uh . . . thanks." Mina took the pastry, feeling queasy at the idea of eating anything at the moment. "You didn't have to do that."

"I wanted to. You have your whole life ahead of you, Mina. Don't waste it . . . here with some of these people."

With a sigh, Mina dropped the pastry and card into her bag. "I don't know where else I'd rather be. I feel closest to Mama here. Thanks again, Sangeeta."

Chapter Three

AFTER CHECKING IN with his mother about his father's health, Hem managed to score a few hours of sleep on his flight back to the States. The only problem was that he didn't have any time to stop at his penthouse for a shower. Instead, he took a car straight from the airport to his father's office, which spread across seven floors of a high-rise on Park Avenue.

As he entered the reception area, he paused, taking in the renovations that his brother had done. During Hem's tenure, the New York headquarters was comprised of gray cubicles and standard boxed offices. Since Ajay took over operations, the space had been gutted and redesigned as an open office workspace. Rows of standing desks were occupied by diligent employees focused on dual screen monitors. In the middle of the floor, clusters of colorful couches and sitting areas were used for conversation and informal team meetings.

Hem had been coming to the office since he was a little boy, but it had been a long time since his father welcomed him at Bharat. Hem had to work at suppressing a mix of nerves and anticipation.

"Can I help you, sir?" a petite older woman said from behind the reception desk. She had to be a new hire that started, what, in the last year or so? Had that much changed since he quit as COO?

"I'm good," he replied and turned left to walk down the hallway.

"Sir! You're not allowed to be here unescorted! I'll have to call security."

"You can call security, but it'll just waste time for both of us. I appreciate that you're doing your job, but I'm the owner's son."

He heard her gasp and suppressed a grin as he continued down the hallway to the large boardroom in the back.

Hem turned the corner and saw his brothers, Ajay and Zail, standing to the left of the double doors wearing custom three-piece suits similar to his and gripping their cell phones. His younger brothers, Hem thought. These idiots were the reason why he dropped everything.

He'd seen Ajay two months ago, and he looked exactly the same. Lean, clean-shaven, and alert. He was almost a direct contrast to Hem's day-old scruff. Zail, his baby brother, had been buried in his lab for the last six months. Not that Hem could tell since Zail's arms were still as thick as a lumberjack's. His beard had grown out, even though it was neat and trim. His hair was longer, too, and he had tied it in a fucking man bun.

A man bun. Their ancestors would've laughed.

"Oh, chutiyae," Hem said. "I made it." Ajay and Zail looked up simultaneously with haunted and relieved expressions on their faces.

"It's been too long, bhai," Zail said as he grabbed him in a bear hug and slapped him on the back. Ajay did the same except with a little more restraint.

"Did you see Dad?" he asked when he pulled away.

Hem shook his head. "I talked to Mom and got an update, but I didn't have time for anything else. I came straight here from the airport. Why are you two standing outside? The meeting was supposed to start ten minutes ago."

"We wanted to go in together. United front and all that," Zail said quietly. "Do you have an idea on how we can address these fuckers? They're going to ask why Dad isn't here."

"What do they know?"

Ajay shook his head. "Absolutely nothing. I've been telling people that Dad is working on something new so he's AWOL this week. I don't know if that'll fly in this meeting, though. The last thing we need right now is for the board to vote to oust Dad. That's the next step after WTA's offer."

"Where's Bill? Legal should be all over this."

"He retired three months ago," Ajay said.

"You're shitting me."

"I wish. We're still reviewing résumés for his replacement. We could've promoted one of the younger employees but they are just too green. No one has the vast experience that Bill had. Other than you, of course."

A rush of cold adrenaline coursed through Hem's veins as an idea formed. Hopefully his instincts would lead him in the right direction. He gripped the door handle.

"I need you to back me up. Follow my lead."

"Done," Ajay and Zail said in unison.

Hem knew that if he created a scene, the board would be focused on him and not the fact that his father wasn't present as the head of the company. He was a majority shareholder who'd been absent from all of the meetings since he resigned from the company, so no one knew how he'd be in a leadership role. That was a plus in his favor.

Fuck all the overthinking, he thought and yanked open the doors with enough force to crash against the walls. The sound was loud enough to silence every person on the floor as well as in the boardroom. He stood by his brothers in the entryway as he scanned the table surrounded by a dozen occupied leather chairs. The wall-to-wall windows displayed the most prominent view of the river, sparkling in the distance.

"Hello, everyone."

There were shocked expressions and rumbles of disapproval from some of the relics in the room. Hem straightened his tie with one hand, strode to the credenza against the far wall, and dropped his briefcase on the oak surface. Ajay and Zail took opposite corners on the other side of the room and stood with arms crossed over their chests.

"Gentlemen?" Ajay said. "Once you've composed yourselves, Hem has the floor."

"How is everyone? I know I'm not the face you expected to see, but I'm the one you've got, so take a good look and enjoy it. You can whisper about me later."

To his left, a leather chair rolled away from the table. "Well, you know how to make a first impression."

That was when he first saw her.

She sat with her legs crossed, wearing a fitted dress that modestly draped over her thighs, hair precariously pinned on the top of her head, large eyes, straight nose, and a pursed mouth made for dirty thoughts.

She was the most beautiful woman he'd ever seen.

It took him a moment to register that everyone in the room was waiting for him to answer her. "I think you're the one who knows how to make an impression."

The woman unfolded her legs slowly and stood. He followed the way her body moved and stretched until she reached her full height. Shit, she was almost eye level with him. Judging by her heels, she had to be six foot without shoes. He loved confidence, and it took a confident fucking woman to give conventions the finger and embrace every inch she had.

"Mina Kohli," she said, extending a hand. "I was chosen to lead your compensation committee and provide a response to the board and major shareholders about the offer."

Hem slid his palm against hers and gripped. Mina's dream-girl eyes widened when Hem squeezed her palm.

Oh yes. This was very interesting.

He let her go when her gaze narrowed at his prolonged hold. "Okay, Mina, why don't you have a seat? You can get started as soon as I'm done. As for the rest of you, thank you for selecting a lead for the compensation committee. Anything else you want to let us know while we're here? Shouldn't you tell us what we should have for lunch? Or how to brush our fucking teeth?"

"Check the attitude, Hem," Frankie Uncle said from the head of the table. He was older than dirt, and the only face in the room that was remotely familiar. Frankie Uncle was a Nobel Laureate and had known Hem since he was in diapers, which meant he'd be the hardest to get in line. "You haven't been at the company in over a year and you waltz back in here making comments about decisions we have to make? That's not how this works, puttar. We have obligations to shareholders now."

Puttar.

Son.

He hadn't acted like one in a long time, thanks to his father's disapproval, but he'd still do right by him.

"No, *this* isn't how it works," Hem said, drawing everyone's attention to him. "I was enjoying a whiskey in Manila when I was asked to come back to Bharat. And why? Because I find out that the board went rogue and made the decision, without management or my father's knowledge, to put together a bullshit meeting. This could've been addressed remote and I could've finished my whiskey and my night."

"Where is your father?" another board member asked. "Sending his thug sons to do his dirty work like a coward?"

Hem calmly straightened his cuffs with diamond cuff links that matched the stud in his ear. "Talk about my father like that one more time and you'll find yourself out of a board seat, a job, and in a precarious financial situation. Depending on my mood, I may just rip your fucking throat out, too."

"Theoretically," Ajay interjected.

Hem grinned at his brother. "Yes, theoretically of course. And like I said, this is an inconsequential meeting. Dad hasn't worked on something new in the last five years but a few weeks ago, inspiration struck. Inspiration that will line all of our pockets like it has for the last three decades."

"He's in the innovation center," Zail chimed in. "He couldn't catch a flight back in time, and I told him not to bother with dialing in."

"And as my brother so eloquently stated," Ajay added, "this is a bullshit meeting. I agreed to Sanjeev's suggestion to use one of his attorneys for the compensation committee, and you all have to vote on three additional chair spots, but no decisions can be made outside that scope without my express approval. Submit your nominations. My father will confirm them and you can go back to relaxing and receiving checks."

"And don't think for a second," Hem said, leaning on the conference table, "that if you try to do anything to jeopardize the health of this organization, my brothers and I will wait patiently on the sidelines."

Hem knocked on the conference table in front of Mina's laptop. "Based on the letter WTA sent detailing the formal offer, you have thirty days, but I made some calls. We got the deadline extended to two and a half months. Our decision is due the week of our next quarterly board meeting."

"I figured you'd do as much, but I'd like to see confirmation of that date change."

"Fine. I expect you to be here in two days, Ms. Kohli. That'll give us enough time to set you and the team up with nondisclosures and clearances. You'll need various expertise to assist you, especially a technical patent—"

"Yes, I know. That'll be me."

"Excellent." He stood to his full height again and nodded to his brothers. They moved to the door and he grabbed his bag to do the same.

"Wait!" Mina said, standing again. "I know that Zail runs R&D and Ajay is COO, but what are you?"

"We want to know that, too," Frankie Uncle said. "You storm in here, ordering us around like you're COO again, but you have no right. You quit, remember?"

"But I'm still a major shareholder, and Bharat's success is in my best interest," Hem said and swung his briefcase strap over one shoulder. "I have a new title to prove it. Interim SVP of Legal at Bharat, Inc." He motioned to Mina with his chin. "Isn't that convenient?"

Hem left the room with his brothers following close behind.

"What was that about?" Ajay asked.

"That was deflection and arrogance," Hem said. "You can tell she's smart just by the way she stood her ground and asked me who I was." *She's fucking gorgeous, too.* "Mina is going to be interesting to work with."

"I agree," Zail mused.

"Stop thinking with your dicks for a second," Ajay said. "I'm talking about your new position here, Hem. You go from COO to interim SVP of Legal?"

"It's the best I could do under the circumstance."

"But is it true?" Zail asked with a grin. "That'll make Dad feel better in no time. The job doesn't require approval from the board, so they have no say in whether or not you can be involved."

"It's temporary, and the only way that these fuckers will accept my presence. It's clear that they want to accept the offer. You can see the hunger on their faces."

Zail's expression darkened. "No one is going to take Dad's business from us. I know you two don't see eye to eye anymore, Hem, but you coming back means a lot."

"You know I'd do anything for the family."

"Right," Ajay said.

They bumped fists in a triad, the same way they'd been doing since they were kids.

It was time to get to work, Hemdeep thought.

Chapter Four

THE BOARD STAYED for another thirty minutes and selected the rest of the committee members to review WTA's offer. Ajay and Zail rejoined the meeting, while Hem touched base with the legal team and made appointments to get up to speed. He came back just in time to see the conference room empty with his brothers leading everyone to the exit. He scanned faces, looking for one person in particular, and when he found her, she was alone and packing her tablet away in a sleek bag while facing the windows and the view.

He'd been too busy setting up his firm, too caught up with work to date for any length of time. And as shallow as it sounded, he avoided women that he could take home to his mother. He'd learned the hard way that his parents were a little too eager to have their sons married to anyone, and a Punjabi bride would make them uncontrollable.

But with Mina, he'd be lying to himself if he said that he wasn't willing to play with fire and get a little closer to her.

"Do you have the information you need?" he asked.

Mina looked over her shoulder, surprise on her face. "Yes. I should be good to go. I'll be in the office first thing next week to get started. I'll need introductions to your legal team—"

"Finance, R&D, and executive leadership, I know."

She smiled and looped the straps of her bag over her shoulder. "Yes, of course you would. I'll email Ajay if I have any other requests."

"We could have a working lunch to talk through anything you may need. I have a little more time to discuss the due diligence strategy. Unless you have someone you need to get back to, of course."

Mina let out a short laugh that was so bright, Hem could've sworn he saw her sparkle. "Is that your not-so-subtle way of asking whether or not I'm available?"

"Man, all the rule books told me that line was practically secret code that only guys knew."

"Nope."

"Nope to if you have someone? Or nope to the secret code part?"

She turned to look at him, and he felt the impact of her stare like a punch to the gut. Those eyes could probably convince him to do anything. Then her perfect mouth curved. "The answer is nope to all three questions. I'm not seeing someone, the secret code is a myth, and I won't have a working lunch with you. I don't think you and I would enjoy the same food."

"Why do you say that?"

She moved to walk past him, and he turned to follow. "Besides the fact that I'm doing a due diligence review for the purchase of your father's company?"

"Well, yeah."

She turned to look over her shoulder, a mischievous glint in her eye. "Anyone who wears a hundred-thousand-dollar suit probably thinks they're too good for my taste."

Hem looked down at his clothes, the only ones he had with him from Manila, and sighed. "I feel like it's cliché to say that you shouldn't judge a book by its cover."

"Then don't," she called out cheerfully as she walked down the hallway.

"What if I told you I knew where you could get the best Indian food in the tristate area?"

"I'm from Jersey. I already found the best Indian food."

"Moghul Express in Edison?"

Mina stopped in her tracks and whirled around to face him, this time with surprise. "Well, well. The man does have taste after all."

"Imagine the work we can get done over bhature chole."

"Their pani puri is also—"

"Amazing," Hem said with a sigh. "See? Our tastes aren't that different after all."

Mina turned and continued walking toward the front doors. "Fine, you do know good Indian food. But it's going to take more than that to get me interested in something other than your financial reports, Hemdeep Singh. I've got too much going on in my life to be distracted by hundred-thousand-dollar suits. Let's keep it professional, shall we?"

She pushed through the glass doors and pressed a button to call the elevator. With one last flutter of her fingers in his direction, she disappeared from view.

Hem clutched a hand over his chest and let out a sigh. Where had that woman been all these years? He'd rarely if ever met someone else who enjoyed Indian street food as much as he did.

"Sir?"

Hem looked over at the receptionist whom he'd scared shitless when he first came in. She held out his coat and bag. Her cheeks were stained red with embarrassment.

"Oh. Thanks. I appreciate this. Sorry for barging in earlier."

"Uh, it's not a problem, sir."

He took his things, left the receptionist beaming, and after a few more words with his brothers, went to do the most important thing on his list for the day.

Visit his mother.

Hem opted to go straight to the family estate in Alpine, New Jersey, instead of his apartment in midtown. He'd moved into his penthouse after the big fallout and he hadn't been back to the estate since. If he was being honest, he missed home. The penthouse used to be a place he stayed after long nights at the office, so it always had a hotel feel to it. Bharat Mahal, the estate, was different. The main house had eleven suites, but Hem's parents wanted to make sure that they provided their children with extended family quarters, so each son had a two-bedroom, two-and-a-half-bath bungalow with two-car garage and finished basement.

Hem wondered if a woman like Mina would appreciate his bungalow. She seemed pretty city, and he'd known another woman with similar tastes that preferred New York over Alpine.

"You're an idiot, Hem," he muttered to himself when he realized where his thoughts wandered.

"Pardon me, sir?" his driver called out through the partition.

"Nothing. Just talking to myself."

Hem opened up his computer and plugged in his ear piece so he could call his client that he'd represented for the Philippines contract. He walked through the deal and then completed some release documents for Bharat.

He finished just as the car pulled through curling

wrought-iron gates flanked by elephants. Bharat Mahal.
He pocketed his phone as he embraced the onslaught of
memories from his childhood . . . and the last time he'd
seen the home.

Crying.

Shouting.

Anger.

There wasn't any laughter anymore, any joy as there
once had been. The grounds were meticulously maintained, but quiet and lifeless.

Hem's phone buzzed and he read the incoming text
message from his mother.

MOM: Aloo Parante khane hain te ghar aja

Of course his mother knew that he was back. And of
course the first thing she'd ask him was to come to the
house if he wanted paranthas. Homemade fried bread
stuffed with potatoes and spice were exactly what he
could use after weeks of hotel food. He typed a quick
reply to let her know that he'd come after his shower.

"Which direction, sir?" the driver said. The gates
had closed behind them and the car idled on the main
road that led straight to his parents' house.

"Take the first left, the third bungalow on the left
closest to the main house."

"Yes, sir."

Hem watched as they passed Zail's place first. It was
painted a soft gray-blue with bursts of purple and yellow

flowers on the front porch. Zail managed the innovation center in California so he didn't keep a place in the city. He used the bungalow as his East Coast residence when he flew out twice a week.

Less than a hundred yards down the lane was a carbon copy home in pale yellow. Ajay's house.

When Hem's bungalow came into view, he felt a pang of sweetness and regret. He was supposed to live in the bungalow with his wife. He'd planned to raise his children there. The mint green colonial with white shutters, maroon pots, and the wind chime Lisa had purchased for him were exactly as he'd left it a year and a half ago.

He got out of the car and circled, seeing the lush gardens spread across the front lawns, the main house in the distance, and the thick forest that enclosed the estate on three sides.

"Thanks, David," Hem said as the driver took the suitcase out of the trunk.

"My pleasure." He left without another word while Hem climbed the front porch and opened the front door.

Sandalwood. Rose incense. Pine.

He felt the ache deep in his chest as he crossed the polished hardwood and ran his fingertips over the plush leather couch that faced a flat-screen TV mounted over a fireplace. He climbed the stairs to the second floor, which had two suites on either side of the hall, and entered the master. All he wanted to do was lie down on the bed and avoid the inevitable, but he couldn't. His mother was waiting for him.

His father was waiting.

Hem made quick work of showering and getting dressed. Instead of walking, he drove his SUV out of his garage and down the drive toward the main house. Bikram Chacha, the estate manager, was standing in the entrance, waiting for him to park at the base of the cathedral stairs.

"Master Hemdeep," he said with a toothy smile. "Long time, long time."

"Bikram Chacha, your English keeps getting better and better."

"I practicing," he said with pride. "Your mom inside. Your dad, upstairs. I see you soon."

"Thanks, Chacha."

Hem slapped him on the shoulder before he kicked off his shoes in the grand foyer. He walked past the dual staircase with curved mahogany banisters, through the great hall, and into the kitchen. His mother stood in front of the oven, humming along with the Punjabi folk songs playing softly in the wall speakers, and the smell of melting ghee and the soft sizzle of stuffed bread on a hot griddle filled the air.

"Muma," he said.

His mother turned, her face marked by the faintest lines of age, brightened with joy. Hem rounded the island and touched her feet, accepting the blessings she always gave him, even when she was mad. Then he snatched her up and spun her in circles like he'd done every time he came to visit her.

"Oy, bewakoof!" She smacked him on the shoulder, even as she laughed and her long black braid whipped around. "My puttar," she said when he finally dropped her to her feet. Her eyes glowed with unshed tears and Hem leaned down so that she could cup his face in her hands.

"Missed you, Muma."

"Of course you did," she said. "My idiot son with his pride. Can't even come home regularly to say hello to his mother."

"But I didn't go a day without thinking of you, so that has to count for something."

She sniffled and waved a hand in the air as if she was swatting a fly. "Tu rehnde. I don't believe your pretty words."

God, she was such a strong woman. She supported her husband when he'd had nothing to his name but a dream and raised a family with an iron fist. Hem lifted her hands and pressed them against his cheeks. Coconut oil and talcum powder. He was home, and it was both joyous and painful.

"Eat and drink some masala chai, Hemdeep," she said in Punjabi. "Then go see your father upstairs."

Hem sat at the island and watched as she picked up a parantha and slid it onto his plate. She added mango pickle, a tab of fresh butter, and two heaps of homemade dahi. The yogurt was tart and cool, the mango pickle fragrant and tangy. The silver kara he wore on his left wrist clinked against the plate as he tore a piece of the bread and felt the flavors explode in his mouth.

He looked up to see her watching him, holding a teacup that matched the one sitting at his elbow. "Mom? How's Dad doing?"

"His heart is broken," she said quietly.

"Is that what the doctor said? Because if he needs a stent or open-heart surgery, I know a few great specialists that can help."

His mother shot him a look before she turned and rolled out the dough for the second parantha. "My oldest baby. So responsible and so literal all the time. No, he has the depression. He feels the shame of losing all he's worked for before it passed to you."

"To Ajay, you mean."

She sighed. "To all of you, Hem."

He nodded. "Are you worried about the company?"

"I worry about our . . . reputation. Bharat was our first success. It's our legacy. All the other businesses mean nothing if we cannot keep Bharat."

"What? Why?"

She shot him an annoyed look over her shoulder as she flipped the parantha. "One a lawyer, one an accountant, and one a software engineer. All of you are executives and among the three of you, no one can figure out why family, legacy, honor, and tradition are the most important parts of your life. Maybe it's because none of you are married and all three in your thirties. Bharat goes, then we'll truly lose respect for any family success."

"Christ, Mom—"

She slammed the rolling pin onto the counter. "We

didn't send you to religious studies at the gurdwara for years so you can come in here saying 'Christ' or 'Jesus!' Show some respect, Hem. All I'm saying is that I saw your brother Zail in a magazine with some girl at a Hollywood fund-raiser party. When I asked him about her, what does he say? That he forgot her name already. So shameless. Your cousins are younger than you and already have children!"

"Yeah, that's because they live in farmhouses in Punjab, Mom. What else is there to do out there besides ride tractors, eat sugarcane, and make babies?"

"Hem, I'm being serious. When are you going to settle down with a nice girl? Lisa was so long ago."

"A year and a half isn't long," he said, praying for patience. His mother was picking at a scab and he knew sooner or later he would bleed.

"Lisa was not right for you. She ran because she couldn't handle a little pressure."

"A little pressure? Mom, I hadn't even proposed and you were showing her wedding venues and save the date cards."

"See? Nothing. How would she have dealt with the extended family?"

"Lisa and I hadn't been dating long enough to deal with extended family—"

"*Two years* is very long, Hem."

"—and you never gave her a chance to adjust! Look, I don't want to talk about Lisa. She's gone just like you two wanted."

"Your sadness is never something we want. But it's in the past, and time for you and your father to let it go. You need someone who can handle the pressure you're under and stand by your side. You need a woman who can interpret both sides of you."

Both sides. The Punjabi and the American side. The traditional and religious part of him that he cherished, versus the corporate business owner.

Was his mother right? Had Lisa ever truly understood all of him? What if she wasn't strong enough, and the reason why she left him was because their differences scared her? A dull ache spread in his chest. Old wounds.

"Let's not talk about this," he said. "Finding the right woman is not my priority right now." He had a fleeting thought of Mina but brushed it aside.

"Hem, you have so much love to give."

"I'll give it to you and my brothers," he said as she slipped another parantha onto his plate. "I know you want Dad to be happy, but marriage isn't the answer. Not right now. However, I think I have something that could work for the company . . ."

She stood on the other side of the island, spatula in hand. "Tell me."

He gave her the full recap of the day's events. Ajay would take the lead, Hem would act as legal, and Zail would be increasing his trips back East.

He could tell that his mother's hope blossomed as he continued to tell her details of the plan.

"Fight them," she said in Punjabi. "Fight WTA and give them back what they did to us, ruining our reputation and almost killing your father. Put them through the same pain."

"We will, Mom."

Hem's mother nodded, taking the empty plate away. "Your father been dealing with so much. His sons are not married, his eldest does not want his birthright, and even his brothers in India are suffering. Your father thinks that your uncle Gopal has been gambling."

"What? I didn't know there were issues."

Hem's mother nodded. "I told your father to bring him out here, get him away from the things that tempt him, but he never got the chance. And now with his heart attack . . ."

"Do you want me to deal with Gopal?"

"No, my bacha. Not now. You have more important things to take care of. Go upstairs and see your father. Find out how he's doing and tell him your news. Then we'll figure out everything else."

Hem kissed his mom's temple before passing her his empty plate, washing his hands at the marble sink, and walking up the wide staircase to the east wing of the house. He opened the last door at the end of the hall and peeked inside. The majestic four poster bed was empty, which made Hem open the door wider in alarm.

He turned toward the floor-to-ceiling windows and saw the older man sitting in a rocking chair facing the gardens outside. A mud-colored shawl was draped around his shoulders and his head was tipped back. He stared blankly at the view of the back of the estate.

"Papa?" Hem said quietly. His heart pounded. This was not how he'd expected his first meeting with his father to go. The paranthas sat heavy in his stomach. The sour words that had passed between them echoed in his head.

His father's head cocked to the left indicating that he was awake. Hem stepped into the room, his bare feet silent on the plush carpet. When he stood in front of his father, taking in the listless expression, the unfocused eyes, his own heart felt like it was breaking. This brilliant, vibrant man was a shell of himself. Hem would give anything to see him burning with fire again, even if that meant he'd be hurt in the process.

"You came to see me," the whispered voice said in Punjabi.

"Of course," Hem said. "Always getting yourself into trouble, right, Papa?"

There was a hint of a smile, and Hem could feel the tears well his throat. "Your mother thinks it's the mango pickle."

"She could be right."

"Don't you know by now? Your mother is always right."

Hem laughed, and the sound was a little watery. He hitched up his jeans and sat on the floor at the base of his father's feet. He rested his elbows on his knees and looked up at the sullen, gray face.

"How is my papa?" he said, putting their angry words and resentment in the past. He reached out and gripped his father's large hand in his.

"Vadiya. My oldest son has come home."

Tears pricked Hem's eyes. "Yes. And I'm working with Ajay and Zail to help you fight WTA for good."

"You're working for Bharat?"

"Consulting. But yes. Focus on your health. Everyone thinks you're designing software so you have time to heal while we take care of things."

"Are you c-coming b-back?"

Hem debated telling his father a lie. There was too much hope in his face, just like his mother's. "I don't think so, Papa."

They sat in silence for a long time. The muffled steps of staff in the halls periodically interrupted their thoughts.

"Shall I tell you something interesting that your oldest discovered today?" Hem said in Punjabi.

That earned a sideways glance, the way it always used to as a child when he promised his father interesting news.

"Sanjeev sent his niece, Mina Kohli, to the meeting today. She looks like a typical sardarni. Long hair, very tall. She's managing the compensation committee that's supposed to deliberate on this dumb offer."

His father turned now to look at him, the haziness cleared for a moment from his eyes. "Are you going to see her again?" he said, his voice heavy with exhaustion.

"Yes, we'll be working together."

The corner of his mouth turned up in the barest hint of a rare, precious smile. "Good."

Chapter Five

MINA HAD SEEN her fair share of beautiful men, but the Singh brothers were in a whole different league. They were like the Punjabis her mother warned her about when she was a child. Their edges weren't just rough, they were serrated. Built, with smooth dark skin and light brown eyes, their masculinity was barely restrained in custom-fit suits.

Especially Hemdeep Singh.

It had been a few days since she'd seen him, but in that time, she'd done nothing but obsess about the way she reacted in the boardroom. It had to be his height.

For a man, height had advantages. For a woman . . . Well, not as much. Mina's made her miserable in her teen years, irritated in her college and law school days, and pissed her off as an adult. Men were always intimidated by her height and assumed that because she was tall, her strength outmatched theirs. The minute she stood up and faced Hem, she knew that he wouldn't have the same insecurity. Even with heels, a tool and a love she'd learned to embrace, Hem towered over her.

Mina gave herself countless lectures on how to avoid focusing on the oldest Singh when she had to start doc review. By the time she reached the Bharat offices for her meeting, she was sure she appeared the image of confidence and control. Mina Kohli was not going to flirt again. Nope. No way, no how. She was going to be completely immune to his charm.

The receptionist greeted her when she was buzzed into the lobby. While she waited for Ajay's assistant to come out to retrieve her, Mina walked over to the framed magazine covers that hung on the wall. All of them featured Deepak Singh's brilliance and the legacy that he was leaving behind, but not one mentioned his sons.

Although Hem, Ajay, and Zail had periodically made it into conference or business news, she couldn't find much about their private lives. Not one had a social media account or even a company distributed headshot. The most current article she found was of Zail's attendance at a Hollywood fund-raiser with an actress, but the piece was focused more on the actress than Zail.

"Ms. Kohli?" a voice said from behind her. She turned to see a young, fresh-faced man holding an iPad in one hand and a temporary badge in the other. "I'm

Mr. Singh's assistant, Rafael. If you'll follow me, he and his brothers are waiting for you."

He led the way down the hall and turned into a corner office. Mina paused at the entrance. The wall of windows overlooked expansive water and cityscape. In front of the windows was a mahogany desk with a high-back leather chair. Clustered in the center of the room were a leather couch and two armchairs surrounding a glass-top coffee table.

Ajay sat behind the desk, Zail sprawled over the couch, and Hem stood. Did they know they looked like three hungry tigers? Lucky for her, she wasn't intimidated by beasts.

Well, not really.

"Gentlemen," she said.

"Mina," Hem replied. "Welcome back."

Mina heard the door close quietly behind her. Within moments, a privacy screen lowered to block out the clear windows and glass door.

"I hope you're all rested after this week's excitement," she said as she crossed the room and sat in the vacant client chair.

"What excitement?" Zail said with a grin. "Here, that's just another typical work day."

"I'm sure. I need to develop a process for our due diligence report, and a list of the documents for each member reviewing your company files. Although I'll only be hands-on with the patent documents and patent applications in progress, I'll still review the findings of both financials and market share analysis reports completed by the other committee members."

"You'll have access to the executives, but everything will go through Hem," Ajay said.

"That's fine." She paused, debating whether or not she should ask her question. When Hem arched one bold brow in her direction, she said, "Do you know why WTA wants to take over the company?"

"It has to do with government contracts they would like to fulfill," Ajay replied.

"You have to give me more than that," she said. "For this to work, we have to be honest with each other."

Hem inched closer. "That is the honest answer. WTA wants to use Bharat's patented software for their military contracts. We found out from our father that there was a preliminary meeting he had with WTA's CEO a few months ago. A one-off encounter. It left a bad taste in his mouth. We don't have any more specifics than that."

Mina thought about what her uncle had said and realized that Sanjeev may have been telling her the truth. Once she got more involved in due diligence, she'd be able to discover the software WTA wanted, but for now, Hem's explanation was enough.

"Okay, then I guess the next thing to take care of is meeting your father. When is Mr. Singh coming back from California?"

The brothers looked at each other again, filling the room with silence.

"This is not a trick question," she said.

"My father is . . . unavailable," Hem replied. "For an undetermined period of time."

"What does that mean? He knows that he has a fiduciary duty to the board in seeing this through, right?"

"He suffered from a heart attack five days ago, and he's on bed rest," Zail added.

"What? Oh my god."

"We're asking you to keep that information to yourself," Ajay said. "If he doesn't improve at the rate his doctors expect, then Hem, Zail, and I will report to the board and the shareholders. But for now, we're not telling anyone. It's too much stress for him and he needs to focus on getting better."

Mina realized the implications of what they were telling her. Shit. They'd put her in a position and they knew it. "Why are you telling me the truth?"

"Because Hem said that we should," Ajay replied. "And Hem is almost never wrong."

"I technically have a duty to the board—"

"You have a duty to the board to review WTA's offer and that's it," Hem said. "We're working together here. We don't know each other right now, don't trust each other, but we have to start somewhere and this is the first step we're taking with you."

He reached out as if he was about to touch her hand. His fingers were long, with the appearance of calloused tips that Mina was itching to feel. Even though he pulled back, the thought of his nearness had her scrambling to her feet.

"Everyone knows your father is the brains of this company," she said as she tried to regain control of her hormones. "Do you have any idea what could happen if he doesn't recover? If there is any reason to accept WTA's offer, this is it."

"Give us the time it takes for you to review the patents and the applications in progress," Hem said. "If he isn't back in the office by then, we'll support whatever decision you make and choose to report to the board."

That's why they looked so determined, so vicious when she saw them for the first time. Their father's heart attack was probably directly related to the offer from WTA. Mina pinched the bridge of her nose, trying to work through the worst-case scenario.

"I . . . appreciate that you trusted me with this information, but you've put me in a difficult position, and you know it. For now, I'll keep quiet, but I need you to let me know the minute something changes. This could affect . . . everything."

"Done," Hem said. He stood as well and motioned to the door.

"Oh, and one more thing. This calls for a favor."

"A favor?" Ajay said.

"Yes. I'm doing you a favor. When the time comes, I'm going to call in a favor of my own. If we're going to trust each other, this is me trusting you to give me your word."

"What kind of favor?" Zail asked.

"Who knows? After this I could need a job, and you'll

have to hire me." She laughed. In truth, her request was more of a gut reaction. All she truly understood was that when it came time to do a takeover of her own, it wouldn't hurt to have the Singhs on her side.

The brothers looked at each other before they all nodded.

"I'll show you to the conference room," Hem said. "Ajay and our CFO, Damany Gordon, will show you the breadth of material to review before and after going public. You'll be alone with him for most of the morning but I'll sit in to field any questions during the afternoon."

Mina shot him a narrowed look. "Your supervision is not just an attempt to get me to eat Indian food with you, is it?"

Hem grinned. "You're the only one missing out. Not only would I be paying, but we'd get Moghul Express."

"You drive a hard bargain."

"Am I wearing you down?"

"I'll let you know." She brushed past him and nearly flushed when he pressed his large hand on the small of her back to escort her out. She felt the familiar rush of desire and she had to focus on putting one foot in front of the other, just to get out of the office without stumbling.

When they stepped into the hallway, her phone rang in her hand. Mina paused when she saw the name on the screen.

"Need to get that?" Hem said.

"Yeah, give me a moment," Mina said absently and answered. "Hello?"

The rich, husky sound of her friend's voice filtered through the phone. "Happy belated birthday, dost."

"Thanks, friend," Mina said. "For a second I thought there was something wrong for you to be calling in the middle of your incredibly busy work day."

"Running a company does have its perks. Like I'm the boss and can do what I want."

Rajneet Hothi and Mina met at a professional minority women's organization when they were fresh out of college. Raj went on to own a multimillion-dollar company, even though not many people knew she was the brains behind her organization.

"I hope I can be in your shoes one day."

"Don't worry, you will. Listen, what's this I hear about you getting engaged?"

"What?" She drew a blank before remembering the immigration law firm merger. "I'm not. It's a lie. How did you—?"

"I have sources and I need the details. Can I buy you birthday drinks tomorrow tonight? We'll go to The Ice Palace."

"The Ice Palace? I don't know . . ."

"I could use some time off with everything going on right now. Come out with me. Let me treat you and we'll kill two birds with one stone and all that."

She sighed. "Fine. But only because it's my—" She

turned to Hem who continued to openly stare at her. "I'll see you tomorrow."

"Figuring out your Friday night plans?" he asked when she hung up the phone. They continued walking down the hallway.

"No . . . not really. It was a friend and mentor of mine."

"The Ice Palace, huh?"

"Yes." Mina smiled at the way he'd openly eavesdropped on her conversation. "It's a little place where hundred-thousand-dollar suits like to go. Don't tell me you haven't heard of it."

Hem shrugged, and his expression became solemn. "I started working here before college and continued for a while after. Then I started my own place. Working a lot has its disadvantages. I usually spend my Friday nights reviewing documents."

"So there isn't anything that could tempt you into going out instead of working?"

Mina regretted the question the moment it popped out of her mouth. Damn it, she wasn't supposed to flirt with him! She had a job to do, and even though he—

"It depends if you're the one tempting me to go." He gave her a heated expression that had her mouth going dry.

"Would you go if I asked?"

"If I say yes, do I get brownie points for honesty?"

"No." She motioned to the empty room. She felt

flushed and that only meant that she needed to get some space, some clarity away from this man. "As fun as this banter has been, in here we are strictly professionals. We have a job to do."

"Professionals. You've used that word before. Is it a personal favorite?"

"Mr. Singh."

"Hem. I feel like we're past formalities now." He hadn't moved any closer, but his laser-focused stare had Mina growing impossibly warmer under his scrutiny. "I'm not going to apologize for being attracted to you, but yes. I'll support you on this project without distractions."

"Damn it, Hem."

"Let's get started, Mina. We'll keep it, as you like to say, professional. For now."

Chapter Six

AFTER TWO DAYS of staring at numbers, projections, and reports while trying to avoid Hem, Mina was ready for a cocktail. She took the first sip from her martini glass and groaned when the smooth liquor slid down her throat. The bite and blend were exactly what she needed after a long week. She scanned the exclusive VIP section at The Ice Palace and wondered if she was the only person there without any intention of going home with someone else.

The club was a two-story renovated warehouse in the meatpacking district. Every wall, surface, uniform, and piece of furniture was in a shade of icy white, gray, or blue. The couches were plush velour, and the waitstaff was barely dressed. The music pumped hot and loud on the first-level dance floor but was a few decibels quieter on the exclusive second floor.

"So how goes the due diligence review for the Punjabi company?" Rajneet asked. "Or is it just one Punjabi that still has your attention?" She sat across from Mina in a dress cut to her navel and slit to her hips. She was bronzed and toned, her hair perfectly tousled, and her lips a deep cherry red. She had a scotch in one hand and wore a golf ball-size diamond on the other.

"I am never like this, Raj. I have too many things on my plate right now to be like this."

"Honey, you've always had too many things on your plate. That's why you don't date. I think a nice distraction is in order."

"Well, he's definitely that. I don't know why but whenever we talk, he's so, I don't know. Intense and charming all at the same time. I'm not used to that."

"When you first mentioned him, the name rang a bell, but I wasn't sure where. I had to do some digging, but I found gossip. You interested?"

"Uh, yes! Please. This man has me so confused and I could use any ammo you have."

Rajneet began ticking fingers in the air like she was writing on a board. "Hemdeep Singh. Graduated Ivy League. Studied computer science but showed an aptitude for corporate law. He started as an associate in his father's company but quickly accelerated in the ranks. He'd been working there since he was fifteen, so just as much hard work as it was legacy. Mysteriously left the company a year and a half ago to start his own firm. Rumor has it that he opposed the company going public and he and his father disagreed to the point where they couldn't work together. There was also a woman involved apparently."

Mina's jaw dropped. A pang of jealousy stabbed her in the chest, and it was so foreign that she didn't know what to do with it. "What—what happened?"

"She left him. She was also a lawyer. They knew each other from school but didn't start dating until a few years ago. I don't think they were at the altar quite yet, but deposits were paid, that's for sure. No one knows for sure why that ended, either."

"Wow, that's . . . well. I'm surprised nothing made it to TMZ or at least *India Abroad*. How did you find this out?"

Raj waved a hand. "It's nothing. Oh, last thing. Some people think the middle brother is the one tanking the company, not his father. He took over after Bharat went public."

After meeting all three Singhs, Mina wasn't sure why the company wasn't succeeding. The employees she met seemed happy and were loyal to the family. The reports showed that they were on the right trajectory. She knew something was going on, and that her uncle was a part of the mess.

"So?" Raj said. "Are you going to tell him?"

"Tell him what?"

"That you plan on getting engaged, Mina. That your uncle is using you as pawn and you're thinking about agreeing to a match made in business bliss."

"I haven't agreed to the arranged marriage yet. And I may not have to. Depending on how this due diligence turns out."

"Mina, do me a favor and say no to Virat. Don't wait for the results on Bharat's case."

"I figured you'd be in full support of something like this."

Across the icy white café table that separated them, Mina saw the regret in Raj's eyes. "Robert and I decided to marry not because we loved each other, but because we knew we'd make good partners in business. He wanted a socialite that could help him network, and I wanted someone who could help me stay in this country while I got my business off the ground. Although my marriage hasn't been terrible since we're both getting what we wanted out of it, it's loveless. Robert and I are friendly, but we're not friends. We work together, but we don't trust each other. He has his business and social schedule, his discreet affairs, while I have mine. Is that something you really want, Mina? An arrangement with contracts? You have so much passion in you, so much fire. Don't let business and your mission for revenge snuff out that light."

Mina drank again, thinking about her friend's words. She admired Raj. So many people questioned her skills, her motives, and her lifestyle. Despite that, she carried herself like a queen, giving the finger to anyone and everyone who dared step in her way. But the stress of having no one to come home to, no one who understood her true passions and hopes and dreams, had to be exhausting.

A man approached their roped-off section. Normally Raj's security would stop him, but he was immediately ushered in.

"Why hello, handsome," Raj said as the man perched on the edge of her seat. He was clean-cut, polished, and a little too soft around the edges.

"Darling," the man said in a crisp British accent. He took her hand in his and kissed it. "It's been too long since you've made an appearance."

"Business calls. This is my friend Mina. It's her birthday. Tell her happy birthday, love."

The man turned to her. His gray eyes nearly glowed, they matched the decor of their surroundings so well. "Happy birthday, love."

"Uh, thanks."

The man stroked a finger down the side of Raj's neck. "The Fire Lounge has our name on it, darling. Can I steal you away and worship you for a bit?"

Mina choked and began to cough.

"Mina, you okay?" Raj said, reaching out and handing her a napkin.

"Fine," she said hoarsely. "Went down the wrong tube."

The British man seemed undisturbed by Mina's interruption. "Darling? The Fire Lounge is waiting."

"Not tonight. I'm here celebrating with my friend."

Mina waved a hand. "No, you should go get, uh, worshiped. I have to leave soon anyway."

"What? It's only eleven!"

"I have no idea what you're doing with the body colonizer," Mina said in Punjabi, "but don't worry about me. I have to get up early and work tomorrow anyway."

"I don't like leaving you. I'm the one who asked you to come out."

"I'm a big girl. Seriously."

Raj leaned down and hugged Mina. "I'll go, but why don't you relax for a bit? I'll leave security here for you in case too many of these pushy types try to bother you. But of course, you know I encourage it, considering your situation."

Mina rolled her eyes and shooed her friend away.

Raj kissed the tips of her fingers and patted Mina's cheek before she disappeared in the crowd. Mina hoped that her friend found some sort of happiness in the brief affairs and indulgences.

She glanced at her watch and the sliver of remaining liquid in her glass. "Happy birthday to me," she said and downed the contents.

"Now that's a terribly sad-looking drink for a birthday celebration," she heard a familiar voice say.

Hem stood next to Raj's security in black slacks and a fitted gray sweater that clung to wide shoulders and biceps so delicious they should be illegal.

"What are you doing here?"

"Trying to relax after a very long week." He glared at Raj's security, and to Mina's shock, the man stepped to the side. In seconds she was enveloped by the scent and presence of the man who'd plagued her thoughts. Instead of taking Raj's seat, he collapsed on the small available space next to her and draped an arm along the back of the sofa.

"What's with the muscle?"

"He's my friend's hire. She sometimes gets a lot of negative attention."

"Oh? Where's your friend?"

"The Fire Lounge."

Hem's eyebrow shot up. "Well, well. You keep interesting company if you know someone who is heading to the windowless, camera-less room."

Mina grinned. "I thought you didn't know about this place."

"I asked around. I'm glad you invited me out."

He may be distracting, but he kept her on her toes, and that was sexy all by itself. "Technically, I didn't invite you. I hinted at an invite."

"Oh? Is that what it was? My mistake. But since I'm here . . ."

"This is the shit people do late on Friday nights when they aren't working?" Zail's voice broke through Mina's trance and she jolted when the youngest Singh collapsed in the sofa across from her. His hair hung loose around his shoulders, and he wore a button-down that fit him just as snugly as Hem's.

"Zail Singh. It's a . . . okay. I didn't expect you to be here, too."

"We can skip the formalities," Zail said with a wave of his hand. "Especially since I'm here as a wingman in case you make him cry. Wow, I can barely hear myself think in this place. People come here for fun?"

The Ice Palace was in full swing and although the VIP section was quieter, the walls practically vibrated from the noise. Mina inched away, trying to create some space between herself and the hot, hard body next to her.

"To be completely honest, it's not my first choice."

"Mine either," Zail mumbled.

"What do you think now that you're finally here?"

"I think I need a drink."

"Hear, hear," Zail said. He pointed to Mina's glass. "Want a whiskey?"

"No, a martini. I don't think I've ever really tried whiskey. Maybe in college once, but it always smelled too strong for me."

The pained looks of horror that flashed across both Hem's and Zail's faces were almost comical.

"What about trying it under the guidance of a whiskey expert?" Hem said. He pressed a hand to his chest. "I can take care of you."

"I'm sure you can," she murmured.

His eyes narrowed on hers, and her breath caught at the hunger she saw reflected in them. "Are you asking for something more than whiskey, Mina Kohli?"

"No, I—no. Whiskey. I'll try just the whiskey for now." She flagged down a waitress even as she fought to control the tingles coursing through her body.

When a woman with leotard-clad hips approached them, Zail took the lead. He ordered three different brands. "And two of each, one neat, one on the rocks. And water backs, please."

The woman nodded before she walked away.

"Why did you order six?" Mina asked.

"Because you need to try a variety to really learn how to drink," Hem replied.

A few moments later, six whiskeys were placed on the cafe table in front of them with three waters. Hem handed her a tumbler and took one for himself. Zail examined two different glasses before opting for whiskey neat.

They held up their glasses and shouted "Maujaa!"

Mina grinned at the Punjabi toast and sipped her drink. The alcohol burned her throat, and the bitterness lingered in her mouth like a bad taste.

"That's . . . not that bad," she said.

"What? It's great! Okay, try this."

Mina shook her head. "Two drinks is my limit." Ever since her mother's accident, she maintained a sober policy. She knew how alcohol destroyed lives.

Hem turned to face her, mouth agape. "What the hell do you mean, two is your limit? When was the last time you went to a Punjabi wedding?"

"Uh, never?"

Zail choked on his second glass.

Two scantily clad women waved at Zail from the next couch over. Their dresses were practically sheer, and they flipped bleached hair and pouted glossy lips. "We could help you with that," one said.

Zail glared and made a twirling motion with his finger. Mina muffled a laugh as they squeaked and immediately turned around in their seats.

"What about a basic desi party?" Hem pressed. "Haven't you had a few drinks at a Diwali celebration? Holi? Any of those."

Mina shrugged. "My mother died when I was a teenager during the time I started taking an interest in parties and friends. When it was just my father and I, we just . . . I don't know, functioned as roommates. I went to school, then law school where almost all of my friends were white, and that was it. I was out on my own. I was too busy studying and then working."

"Okay fair enough. What if you try it out? I promise I won't let anything happen to you if you do."

She saw the sincerity in his face, and after a moment of reminding herself that this was different than the situation her mother had been in, she held out a hand to Zail.

"Suck another one down, Kohli," Zail said. "It's time to be educated. Try it on the rocks."

She had to admit, she was curious how whiskey neat tasted. She wasn't driving, and if she really needed rescuing, Raj would come out of the Fire Lounge. Mina took another, pausing to enjoy the feel of Hem's hand rubbing the small of her back. She looked at him and raised her glass.

"Maujaa," she said.

Hem grinned and repeated the toast before downing his own drink.

Mina did the same, and this time, the burn was a welcome, warm sensation. It tasted different. Smoother this time.

"Guys? I think I like whiskey," she said.

"Another round then." Hem moved closer to her, and she relaxed against his side. His smell was intoxicating and she enjoyed it like a heady drug while more glasses were placed in front of them.

"Is this what you brothers do together?"

"When we get together these days, it's usually business, but every now and then we like to finish a couple bottles, yes."

"A couple *bottles*?"

Hem brushed a curl over her shoulder and cupped the back of her neck. "A couple bottles, Mina."

She shivered under his touch and watched Hem's eyes darken. Before he could lean in, which was exactly what he looked like he wanted to do, a waitress placed six more glasses in front of them.

"This one has peach nectar, and this has cherry." She motioned to Mina. "If you're more of a flavored martini drinker, this might be to your taste."

Zail waved a hand. "Oh, she won't want that—"

"I do. Thank you," Mina said. When the waitress left again, she turned to Zail. "Don't ever think you can speak for me."

The youngest Singh held his hands up. "It tastes gross with that stuff in it but if you want that garbage, you're more than welcome to it."

Mina reached for the peach one first. "Maujaa!" she shouted and tilted the glass back. The bitterness was dulled by the rich, juicy taste of fruit nectar. "Oh my god, this is *amazing*."

"Oh shit," Hem said.

She wiggled closer to him as he rubbed her arm in long delicious strokes. Her thoughts were beginning to get fuzzy. She wasn't this forward, this obvious with men ever, but with Hem, it was so natural.

"Why don't you slow down before you try the next one? Want to order some food?"

"What, isn't this what you said you guys do? Isn't this how the Punjabis drink?"

"Yeah, but it usually involves conversation, too. Not just who can down the most juice the fastest," Hem said.

"I'm not really that hungry, so why don't we talk? Do you speak Punjabi, too? Or do you only toast in the language?"

Hem pressed his lips to the shell of her ear and her eyes practically rolled back at the soft heat of his breath. "What do you think?" he said in her language.

She had to squeeze her thighs together and bit her lip

to hold back the groan. His voice, plus their language, was pure sin.

She needed some distance. She still had to work with Hem, and as much as she loved every touch, every brush of his hand, and every word, she was getting too light-headed to make sound decisions. "Let's have another."

"Shit, man," Zail said when Mina snatched the cherry-flavored whiskey out of his hand and tossed it back.

"Maujaa!" she shouted and slammed the glass down on the table. Her body felt like it was melting now. Mina shook her hair out of her face. The buzz felt wonderful. Hem's close proximity to her felt wonderful, too.

"Let's have another!" she said, and while Hem and Zail argued with her, she managed to get the waitress to replace her drinks.

She asked them to tell her their favorite whiskey stories, distracting them as she enjoyed the sweet bitterness that stung the tip of her tongue and coated her throat. As the brothers spoke, she could see the love they shared with each other, the humor that came with childhood memories. At one point, Zail threw ice cubes at his brother for recounting the time after he drank too much, he got sick and then their mother chased him with a rolling pin.

After half an hour, Zail stood and motioned to the stairs.

"I'm going to bail," he said. "I don't think you both are going to last much longer anyway, and this place gives me a headache. Next time, let's meet in an actual bar. You okay taking her home, bhai?"

Mina shot up in her seat. "I beg your *pardon*, Zail Singh. I am right here and I can take care of myself just fine." She grabbed her fifth—or was it sixth?—drink and tipped it back. She could barely taste it now. Her body was singing with so much feeling.

"Take care, sweetheart," Zail said and leaned down to press a kiss on her cheek. "See you in the office." She could feel Hem's growl deep in his chest, like he was a damned animal.

"What was that?" she asked him after Zail slipped through the crowd.

"I didn't like it that he touched you."

"Really?"

"Hell, Mina, you don't have to sound so giddy about it."

"It's just so . . . cute."

Hem grinned, and he stroked a fingertip over her knee and teased the skin under the hem of her short dress. "I don't share."

"I'm not a *thing* to share. Man, this is why avoiding dating is so much easier than dealing with man-babies. Now don't get all grumpy just because your brother gave me a smooch."

"Wait, wait, wait. Back up. You don't date at all?"

"Well. Sometimes, but it's too hard to juggle a man-baby and a job. Also, I'm tall and speak my mind. It tends to piss people off." She pointed to her crotch. "Which is why it's just me and B.O.B. The battery-operated purple boyfriend of joy."

"Goddamn, Mina."

"Let's cheers again, Hem," she said cheerfully. "Maujaa!" This time, when she swallowed the whiskey, it felt thick and greasy in her stomach. She pressed both hands to her waist and groaned.

"Mina? You okay?"

"I don't know."

"You've been drinking pretty fast for the last, what, hour? Why don't we slow down for a bit? I'll get you some water to drink."

Mina nodded and slumped against the couch. All thoughts of sex and seduction dissipated as her skin grew clammy. Was this what drinking a lot was supposed to feel like? Didn't it take longer than, what, seven or eight drinks?

The nausea hit fast and furious. She'd only been downing whiskey for a short period of time. Granted, she hadn't eaten a lot of food, but that shouldn't make *too* much of a difference, right? Bile rose like a bubbling pot ready to overflow.

Fuck it, even her fog-brain could register that there was no graceful way to get out of her current predicament now.

"Hem? I'm going to throw up."

A few seconds later, she vomited all over her dress, the couch, and Hem's shoes.

Chapter Seven

IF HEM HADN'T gone out to see Mina the night before, he would've treated his Saturday like any other day of the week. He'd wake up at 4:30, run or lift weights, shower, and then talk to his legal assistant about open action items. Since his last few meetings with Ajay, he'd taken on more of the family business projects, such as their award-winning vineyard and their European hotel so he could alleviate his brother's workload. Unfortunately, that meant he was significantly busier than usual.

All of the things he had to do were nowhere near as distracting as the woman in his bed. Hem looked over at the rumpled sheets where Mina slept in one of his shirts. He sat on the armchair in the corner of the master suite, laptop in hand, and watched her wake, increment by slow increment.

She sat up and pushed her rioting curls out of her face. She was beautiful, even after the eventful night they had. Her makeup was long gone, and her skin looked a little tired, but there was no hiding the fact that she could make him weak.

He was not a weak man.

"Hem?"

He put his laptop on the coffee table and stood. She looked a little bleary-eyed but clearer than he expected after the amount of drinks she'd inhaled. "Morning, sunshine."

Horror crossed her face, and Hem bit back a smile. She remembered what happened.

"I can't believe I vomited all over your shoes."

"Side table. Advil."

She looked over and dove for the pills like they were a lifeline. She tossed it back and then guzzled water like she'd been in the desert for three days.

Hem crossed to her and sat on the edge of the bed within touching distance. When she finished her water, he took the glass and set it down, then caught her fingers in his. Long, slender fingers with nude polish. He reached out and stroked her cheek with the other hand, surprised when she didn't push his hand away.

"How are you feeling?"

"Better than expected for my first time getting drunk. Maybe my Punjabi genes came through."

"Headache?"

She tilted her head side to side, as if waiting for the

pain to rattle around and settle in. "Yes, but a small one. Strange."

"You probably did yourself a favor by throwing it all up last night."

Mortification crossed Mina's face and she pressed a hand to her cheek. "You and that poor waitress—"

"She got a big tip for helping clean you up."

"And then you took me here because—"

"I didn't want you home by yourself in case you got sick again. So I helped you brush your teeth. You handled changing, even though it took you twenty minutes, and I tucked you in to bed. See? I told you I'd take care of you."

Mina's cheeks tinted with the slightest hint of pink under her light brown complexion. "And where did you . . . ?"

"I slept here. Just in case you needed anything."

Her expression relaxed into one of amusement. "That is so typical, Hemdeep Singh. Your Punjabi genes demand that you protect me even though I've never been a damsel in distress. I could've managed, you know."

"I know," he said. "But where we're going in our relationship, I think it's safe to say that I'm going to keep trying to make you happy and keep you safe." Maybe his words seemed a little more forceful than they should've, because she sobered. He hated to see her tense, the way she pulled back from him as if the next steps between them weren't a natural progression of the night before.

"I should probably go home."

Hem stood, admiring the view she made in his t-shirt, surrounded by white bedsheets and comforter. She looked comfortable, and damn it if he didn't want to crawl into bed next to her. But he couldn't. Too soon for her. Too fast. He'd rushed Lisa into a committed relationship, and he'd lost her. The attraction he felt for Mina was so much more, so much stronger than the slow burn he'd experienced before. He wanted this woman, and he had to be careful with her.

"I knew you needed some new clothes to wear in the morning, so I borrowed my brother's personal assistant to help. He's apparently a magician and was able to buy a few things for you. He dropped them off an hour ago. They're in the bathroom. Why don't you get ready and join me in the kitchen for breakfast when you're ready?"

She gaped at him. "You had a personal assistant shop for me?"

He nodded. "My first plan was to get your real clothes, but that didn't work out."

"What? Why not?"

"Long story short, your friend Rajneet called while you were passed out in my car, so I picked up. I explained what happened and asked her if she had a key to your place since there wasn't one in your bag. She said you had keyless entry and didn't have your code, but she did, however, know your size. Raj also threatened me if I didn't take care of you. Scary woman."

The corner of Mina's lip quirked. "That's Raj."

Hem nodded and turned to leave.

"Hem. Thanks. Really."

"Don't mention it."

He was almost at the door, laptop in hand, when she called his name again. "Hem?"

"Yeah?"

There was a long pause, and he saw a flicker of something akin to need on her face. She shook her head. "Nothing."

One minute he was standing across the room, watching her unsure expression and the cloud of hair tumbling over her shoulders, the next he was tossing his laptop on the armchair and striding to her. Her mouth formed a perfect O when he climbed onto the bed. He prowled toward her, and his pulse jumped when she quickly grabbed onto his shoulders and pulled him close.

Hem's mouth claimed Mina's, and the intense sweetness of her lips was like a release he hadn't known he wanted so desperately. He lowered his body to press her into the mattress. His spiking lust fractured his thoughts. Mina's arms wrapped around him, and she pulled the back of his T-shirt up to rake her fingers from shoulders to hips. His erection grew full and thick. The kiss turned rough and he was desperate to feel her skin to skin instead of the fucking blanket that blocked him from her soft, supple skin.

God, he wanted her. He stroked his tongue over hers and swallowed her gasp of pleasure, before pulling back. He had to stop. She was so sweet. He nipped her swollen lip, even as she lifted up, trying to keep his mouth on hers.

"Get dressed," he said, vaulting off the bed.

"What?" she said breathlessly.

"Get dressed, Mina," he repeated. "Unless you want to be fucked. Hard."

He strode out without another backward glance. If she called him again, if she looked at him with the need that mirrored his, he wouldn't stop until they were both done.

Even though the attraction was nuclear, what Mina and Hem shared was new. Hem wasn't used to it. His last relationship took years of friendship before it progressed, and even then, it was built with boundaries. These feelings he was experiencing were uncharted territory for him, and he didn't want to mess things up when there was a chance that it could be so much more than he'd ever had before.

MINA WAS SO turned on that she sat for a full five minutes in a daze after Hem walked out. He'd just . . . left. She would've completely let him have his way with her, but instead, he'd walked out. She touched her swollen mouth and let out a ragged breath.

"Holy shit, Hemdeep Singh."

Never in her life had she been kissed with that much focus, so much passion that her head spun. And she had to work with him for the next two and a half months.

How was she going to handle seeing him in the office, wearing his restrained suits, and not imagine the rough fucking he'd promised? She had to think about something else, something less sexy, so that she could get dressed and put some distance between them.

She looked down at the soft cotton shirt she wore and smelled the lingering scent of spice and man.

The memory of projectile vomit was enough to tamper the effects of the kiss. Yup, she'd been sick everywhere in a public place.

"And now, it's time to get up, Kohli."

Mina pushed the plush comforter aside and crawled out of the California king bed. Sunlight streamed through the wall windows, stinging her eyes a bit as she stretched. For the most part, she had a bucket load of embarrassment and a few aches. And now, wet panties.

Vaguely remembering the penthouse layout from the night before, she crossed to pocket doors that opened to the bathroom. Every gleaming surface was white marble with veins of black and gray. The tiled floor was a rich black with flecks of silver. Mina spotted shopping bags sitting on the end of the countertop that stretched across one wall. Her replacement clothes.

"Oh my god," she said when she began emptying the bags. Inside was a La Perla lace balconette bra and matching thong in her size. It was a beautiful lingerie set, and although she'd indulged in La Perla before, her sets were pretty basic and reserved for special occasions.

A vivid cobalt blue V-neck sundress with a swing

skirt was next, and then a pair of wedge heels with blue-and-white polka dot fabric ankle ties. She stroked her hand over the shoes and the dress for a moment before taking out the hair and skin products from the second bag. Ajay's assistant had thought of everything.

She had to pay Hem back. Two people who weren't in a relationship yet should not be buying each other expensive lingerie and scented creams. For Mina, there was too much riding on her due diligence work at Bharat, Inc., for her to be sidetracked by a man, even if that man was someone like Hem.

She stared at her dull complexion in the mirror for a moment before she tackled brushing her teeth and then washed the rest of the grime away in the glass-enclosed rain shower. She French-braided her wet hair into submission and then left all the products she used in one of the bags. She couldn't justify taking them with her.

She passed two bedrooms and a half bath all exquisitely decorated before she entered the living space. She let out a sigh as she took in the most beautiful great rooms she'd ever seen. The glass wall overlooking Manhattan was a full two stories. A circular couch faced a gas fireplace with a large flat screen mounted over the mantel. The kitchen and a bar station fit in the back corner of the penthouse, featuring a curved marble island. The rich scent of coffee filled the room, and the built-in oven light illuminated a foil tray. The spicy scent of Indian food—paranthas maybe?—filled the air.

"The penthouse loft is pretty sweet, but the kitchen island is what sold me on this place."

Mina looked up to the second story where and Hem leaned over the edge of a half wall.

"You bought a penthouse with two-story views of midtown because of the kitchen *island*?"

He started down the spiral stairs to the main level. "And the rooftop terrace. Oh, and the private parking. This place was my first investment but it became my permanent living quarters recently. Did Ajay's assistant pack everything you need?"

"Like you don't know," Mina said with a smirk.

"Know what?"

"About the La Perla, Hem."

His gaze heated as he approached her like a stalking predator. "It's better if you show me. Just so I know it fits correctly."

She held up a hand like a traffic cop. "Wait! First, let's address the underwear."

"That's what I'm trying to do."

Mina laughed. "No, seriously. You cannot be purchasing designer lingerie for me. It's presumptuous."

"Technically, I didn't," he said with a shrug. "I just told Rafael to get you whatever women need, and he's the one who purchased the lingerie."

"Hem."

He held up his hands in surrender. "Fine, I admit that I like the idea of your clothes here. Of buying clothes for you. I dated someone a while back who would've gone to war with me if I so much as purchased a T-shirt for her and we'd dated for years."

Mina winced. That was a little extreme. She'd definitely accept more than a T-shirt as a gift after a few years of dating, but Mina didn't know Hem's ex-girlfriend, so she wasn't going to pass judgment that quickly. At least not out loud.

"Look, we need to have a discussion about this *thing* between us. About what happened last night and . . . and this morning."

He hesitated, then took her hand to press a kiss to her knuckles. "Okay. Want some coffee? Or are you a chai person?"

"Uh, I'd normally be okay with coffee but if you have chai, I won't turn it down."

He raised an eyebrow, before heading over to a cabinet close to the oven. He pulled down a canister of what looked like loose-leaf tea. With deft efficiency Mina didn't know he possessed, Hem put a pot of water on the stovetop to boil. He also took out a mug, a strainer, ginger, and sugar.

"I'm impressed," she said. "Your mother taught you well."

"My nani, actually. We used to go stay at her farm-house outside Chandigarh during the summer months when we were boys. She said that the one thing she always wished for was a husband who would bring her a cup of chai on occasion, not the reverse, so she taught us all how to make it."

"I think I still have distant relatives in Amritsar, but I'm not sure. My father stopped speaking with his family because he had a love marriage, not an arranged one."

"How long has it been since you've visited India?" Hem asked.

"I went with my mom and dad when I was a kid and haven't gotten a chance to go back since. I keep up the Punjabi because it's important to know what the hell my uncles are talking about when they think no one else is looking."

Mina rounded the island and hoisted herself up so she could sit and watch him more closely. He grated the ginger as if he'd done it a thousand times and added it to the water. When it began to simmer, he poured in three tablespoons of the loose-leaf tea, along with a teaspoon of masala that he pulled from a steel canister. It smelled like cardamom and cloves.

Hem walked over to the custom-designed fridge and took out a glass bottle of milk.

"What?" he said, shooting her a look as he put the milk back.

"Nothing."

"Somethings on your mind, hiriye."

Beloved.

The endearment rocked her. Now was probably the best time to talk about why they didn't belong together, at least not while they worked together. There was too much riding on her decision to get sidetracked. She wanted partner, damn it.

"Hem, I know that you came to the club last night because I sort of initiated the invite. I'm not going to lie. I'm attracted to you. But maybe we should keep things professional, at least until I'm done working at your father's company. Our involvement could be considered a conflict of interest."

He placed the cup of chai next to her and Mina sighed at the scent rising from the steaming caramel-colored liquid.

"Want some breakfast, too?" Hem asked. "Paranthas and aachar."

"Seriously?"

"Absolutely."

"Damn it," she said with a groan. "How am I supposed to tell you to stay away when you're trying to seduce me with food?"

He turned from the stove and placed his hands on her knees. Heat pooled at the juncture of her thighs when he slowly pushed her legs apart and stepped between them. His hands were at her waist, and he looked up at her, his dark stubble giving him a rugged, sexy appeal. She couldn't help herself, as she curled a hand around the back of his neck.

"Mina. First, tell me honestly, are you interested in me or not?"

"We met a week ago!"

"And we don't have to go to the gurdwara today and get married. Are you attracted to me?"

"That's not the point—"

He squeezed her hips and yanked her forward so that her pelvis was flush against the hard ridges of his abdomen. "Tell me the truth," he said. "Do. You. Want. Me."

"Of course I do, damn it, but it doesn't matter!"

He relaxed his hold and dropped a kiss on her collarbone. His stubble tickled the softness of her skin, and she had to hold back a sigh.

"It matters. We'll be professional in the office and we'll take some time to know each other. But I want you, Mina. And if you want me, too, then we're going to happen."

"I have too much riding on my role at Bharat for my personal life to interfere." She tugged his hair at the nape of his neck, and her fingers flexed instinctively in the thick, lush texture of his waves. She couldn't help brushing her thumb over the diamond stud in his earlobe.

"What do you mean by that?" he said, his voice hardening.

Shit. She wasn't ready to tell him that she was trying to find out if her uncle was sabotaging Bharat's offer. She needed more time to do some investigative work before she came clean to Hem and his brothers. If her uncle had a mole and was purposely affecting Bharat's performance, she wanted to be the one to uncover it.

"I mean," she said, stretching out her pronunciation, "that my uncle is on your board of directors, and if I screw up, my chances of becoming partner will be slim to none."

"How about we let things progress, but we'll keep it out of the office? We'll keep this between us. Deal?"

"I'll think about it," she muttered.

He leaned forward and nipped her bottom lip. She let out a gasp and couldn't help but lick the skin that he'd pinched with teeth. He didn't notice since he was too busy taking the foil tray out of the oven.

She pressed her thighs together and tried to control her lust as she watched Hem assemble two plates with mango pickle and what looked like mehti paranthas. She'd always loved the smell of mehti paranthas, even though when she was a child, her mother made the fenugreek seeds ingredient into a paste and forced her to put it in her hair every Sunday so she'd have soft curls.

"Why don't you grab your plate and chai?" Hem said. "We'll eat on the terrace. I'll even let you lecture me some more."

She hopped off the counter, eager to see the view even though she knew she had to maintain the distance between them. Mina picked up her plate and Hem smacked her butt cheek.

"Hemdeep Singh!"

He grinned, the mischievous sparkle in his eyes already dulling her annoyance. "Just making sure you're really wearing the thong."

"You see, *this* is what I'm talking about," she said as she stepped aside so he'd lead. "Are you seriously going to avoid this kind of behavior once we're at Bharat headquarters? I doubt it."

"Hiriye, I'm a sardar. A Punjabi Sikh man. Do you really think I can resist a challenge?"

"And I'm a sardarni," she snapped. "Do you really think I'll put up with your bullshit?"

He leaned forward and stole a quick kiss. "Challenge accepted."

Chapter Eight

SPENDING TIME WITH Mina meant engaging in a constant battle of wit and lust. After breakfast, he'd agreed to drop her off back at her condo, even though he wanted to spend the day with her.

It was probably a good thing they cut their time short. When he went home, Hem began his own due diligence review. It wasn't that he didn't trust Mina to make a fair assessment. His instincts about people were incredibly sharp and he strongly believed that she wouldn't screw him over. But somehow, WTA had managed to surprise them, and he and his brothers had to find out what they were doing wrong.

By Monday morning, he walked into his brother's office with a clearer understanding of what was happening to their company's profit margins and reputation.

"I have some answers for you," Hem said as he collapsed in one of the chairs across from Ajay's desk.

Ajay put down the tablet he was reading and straightened the silver kara he wore on his wrist. "I want to hear about this weekend first."

"That's what I'm about to tell you, asshole."

"Nope. I'm not talking about your reading material. I'm talking about who you were with while you were reading it."

Hem swore. "Zail is a little tattletale bitch."

"Rafael."

"Damn it—"

"And Zail. Did you seriously expect him to keep quiet about that?" Ajay said with a laugh. "Is it true? Did you get Mina drunk and then take her home? Please tell me you were a gentleman until she sobered up."

Hem thought of the rough, barely restrained kisses they'd shared. "She doesn't want us to happen . . . at least not while she's working on Bharat's due diligence review."

"Oh poor baby," Ajay said. "I bet the rejection hurts like a bitch."

"Blue balls are a great motivator. I spent all weekend looking at the company records, and I have a theory. We're going to have to do a lot more work to prove it, but I'm pretty sure I know why we're losing money."

Ajay's teasing expression sobered immediately. "Tell me," he said; his voice became hard and cold as ice.

"Before the company went public, the sales teams were winning seventy-nine percent of the requests for proposals that came in. After the company went public, within six months, the sales team's success with RFPs dropped to less than forty-eight percent."

Ajay's face turned thunderous. "Is this a commentary on my leadership?"

"No. I told you once, and I'll tell you again, you were made to lead this company. You were made to lead all of the Singh companies." Hem knew that people had given Ajay shit, and Hem also knew that for all the pride Ajay possessed, he'd step down if Hem wanted the top spot again. There was no way that would ever happen, but Hem didn't have time to soothe his brother's ego every time they spoke.

"Then why are you looking at the sales numbers?" Ajay grumbled.

"Because absolutely nothing changed from before Bharat went public. We've beat all the big boys. Google. IBM. WTA. But now, for some reason, WTA's shell companies and subsidiaries are winning accounts that should be ours."

Hem took out his laptop and flipped it to tablet mode. In seconds he pulled up the analysis report and slid it across the desk.

"Son of a fucking bitch," Ajay hissed. "How the hell did this happen?"

"WTA has been sneaky about outbidding us on sales opportunities. It looks like random accounts for varying contract values, so you can't really see a trend. Unless you're specifically looking for WTA subsidiaries."

Ajay stood, his movements jerky as he began to pace in front of the window. "The board is way too excited about the offer. Do you think some of them are also involved in trying to take down the company?"

"Could be. Mina's uncle and a few others look like they were salivating at the offer letter."

"Hem, do you think Mina's dirty, too? I know you're thinking with your dick, but I need your brain to be working right now. I can pull her."

"No," Hem said. "And I'm not thinking with my dick when I say that. We need more information and the fastest way to get it is to let Mina do her job."

Ajay collapsed in his chair. He was so much like Hem, and yet they were so different. They needed to figure out a way to make their strengths and weaknesses work together. If WTA had a mole, it was a good one and had gone undetected for months. He needed his brothers to start thinking out of the box.

"Keep an eye out on Mina," Ajay said. "I like her so far since she's managed to keep Dad's secret, but we can't take any chances."

"I know. We need to tell Zail the news. I feel like this affects him, too. Two of the bids that went out included prototype software information from our R&D team out in California. No one else should even be close to developing something like that, yet WTA undercut us on both opportunities."

"This is a shit show," Ajay said, rubbing his hands over his face. "After this is all done and you go back to your firm, we're going to need to beef up the legal team. I can't even imagine the number of lawsuits we're about to enter. Corporate espionage, trade secrets, you name it."

The comm unit on the desk beeped and Ajay pressed the answer button. "I'm in the middle of something, Rafael."

"Sir, your brother and your cousin called. They both would like to telepresence into the unit in your office. I can schedule them individually or together in a group conference at a later point if you'd like."

Hem shifted toward the screens on the far wall and motioned to them. Since the bids were for the US military, Hem didn't even think about the London offices and whether the mole could've hurt business dealings on an international scale. Maybe giving Brahm a heads-up would prevent any further damage to the business.

"Rafael," Ajay called out. "Tell them to call the telepresence line. And if you could set up the unit in here, we'll take their calls now."

"Yes, sir."

Rafael entered the office a few seconds later and walked over to the Polycom unit. He programmed the screens, and when the first call came in, Rafael answered.

Hem grinned when his cousin's face filled the screen. A partial view of the London skyline was visible from the windows behind him. He was also suited up, but unlike Hem and his brothers, Brahm had a bit more style. He was slimmer but just as tall. His face had chiseled edges and facial hair cut with sharp edges in a style that was distinctly European.

"Rafe," Brahm said with warmth. "You look even more gorgeous each time I see you."

"Mr. Singh," Rafael said. His voice was tinged with frost. "Is the audio adequate on your end to continue the call?"

Brahm responded in Spanish. Rafael gave a sharp retort and made a visible motion of muting the screen. The second call came in moments later and Rafael asked the same question to Zail, who was calling in from the California office. Zail nodded.

"The call is ready for you," Rafael said and handed Ajay the remote before exiting the room and closing the door.

"Oye kiddha," Brahm said before switching to his crisp Cambridge accent. "How are my brothers from my other mother doing? Isn't that what Americans say? Hem! Ki haal hai? What the hell are you doing in the office, man? Visiting or begging for your job back? I knew you couldn't hack it in the real world. No one to wipe your ass for you, I'm afraid."

Hem shot his cousin the middle finger. "You're in a cheerful mood after Ajay's assistant turned you down so quickly. You should've taken the offer when he first flirted with you at last year's holiday party."

Brahm grinned. "I was focused on work then. Now?

Let's just say that the Jack Frost impression is even more of a turn-on."

"Yeah, why don't you go back to Punjab and tell the other uncles and our six cousins that you found your Bollywood hero?"

Brahm waved his hand in dismissal. "I've got better things to do than deal with those homophobic alpha-fools. Is your dad there? He hasn't been answering emails."

"Send them to me," Ajay said. "Brahm, we need to tell you something, but you can't leak it to the family. Not your mother, your father, no one."

Brahm's face grew solemn. "Done. What's going on?"

"Dad had a heart attack after WTA's offer came in," Zail said from the adjoining monitor. "We've been covering and now you have to as well."

Brahm's coloring became gray, his eyes wide. "Is Chacha . . . Is he okay?"

"Doctor said he's going to have a full recovery, but Hem is consulting as our legal advisor and Zail has to spend more time on the East Coast."

"Shit," Brahm said, pinching the bridge of his nose. "This is bad. Especially since Gopal is on a fucking bender and causing problems. It's gotten worse, probably because Deepak isn't there to take care of him. He needs to be . . . addressed."

"Mom mentioned that he got into a bit of gambling," Zail said.

"That's an understatement. Our law enforcement connections in the area have confirmed that he's now indebted to one of the drug lords that kills first and asks question later."

Hem swore. If his uncle owed money to a drug lord, then the price for repayment would be extreme. Regardless of the family's connections to law enforcement, the drug cartel in Punjab was no joke.

"How do we smuggle him out?" Zail asked.

"I can get him out," Brahm replied. "But it'll have to be a stealth mission."

"Shit," Ajay said. "That means he's in deep."

"Very, bhai. Very. If you're acting as your father, then give me a week and I'll have Gopal in detox here in the UK."

"Thanks, Brahm," Hem said. "We owe you one."

Brahm lifted a white teacup and sipped. "A raise would be nice. Now that conversation is dealt with, in addition to the news on my favorite uncle's health, none of you fuckers debriefed me on last week's impromptu board meeting. Whatsapp messages don't count. What the hell is going on over there? Am I going to have to pray for another family member to get rich and secure my employment at a London office? That's damned inconvenient."

"No one's getting rid of you yet, British boy, but we do have a problem." Hem walked through his weekend discovery one more time for Zail and Brahm. The joking was quickly put aside and Hem watched their expressions cloud with the anger that had been sitting inside him.

"I'll get our cyber security team on it," Zail said. "They'll have to search computers and email accounts. If there is a tiny slipup from any of the employees, my teams will find it. I know that the security work is already overflowing, so if we need to hire more heads, let's start the process now."

"We won't need bodies over here," Brahm said. "But if I have to clean house, I will. Deepak worked too hard for his company. And Hem? Mina's decision could end this in either a good or bad way. She holds the key. Watch your back, bhai."

Zail scratched his facial hair and cleared his throat. "Hem, I have a suggestion that you're not going to like."

"What is it?"

"I know you want to sleep with her—"

"Zail—"

"So if you finally convince her that you'll wear a paper bag over your head and your dick isn't two inches—"

"I'm going to kill you, Zail."

"—then why don't you do a little forensic investigation on her? Get one of the security teams to dedicate some time on her background, her uncles, the firm, everything. If she suspects that she's being watched, you'd have already earned her trust by then."

Hem hated the idea of lying to Mina, but at the same time, he knew that his brother had a point. He trusted his gut, but there were too many jobs relying on Mina's decision for Hem not to be a little cautious. "I'll think about it."

"Think fast," Ajay said. He pointed at his tablet. "Rafael said she's here and he's going to set her up in a conference room near the senior managers in the finance team. You'll have to go downstairs to see her."

Hem stood and straightened his tie. "Brahm, let us know if you need us to provide additional support for Gopal's extraction. And instead of paying the drug lord, let's pay our connections to get rid of the bastard so he doesn't come back and make things difficult for the family."

"On it, brother."

Thankfully, his family wasn't squeamish about the dirty work. Punjab was not like the United States. Sometimes, corruption needed to be dealt with through vigilante justice, not through a court system. He waved at Zail and turned to leave when Ajay called after him. "Where are you going?"

"I'm getting Starbucks."

Brahm, Zail, and Ajay all gave him puzzled expressions. "Why don't you send someone to get it for you? That's why you're rich, chutiya."

"Because knowing Mina, she'd reject anything I didn't get myself."

All three men in the room burst out laughing. Hem gave them the finger and walked out, but he could still hear them cackling and making whooshing sounds like a whip as he walked to the elevator.

He was *not* whipped. He was . . . being strategic. If he was going to get Mina to let him into her bed, he had to follow her rules. Her quick wit kept him on his toes, and her sense of humor tore down his barriers. To have a chance with her, he needed to be two steps ahead.

He was halfway through the lobby doors when he realized that it had been so long since he'd ordered from Starbucks that he'd probably make a fool of himself if he didn't do some recon first. He called Mina's office and asked for her assistant. A cheerful woman answered.

"Hi, this is Hemdeep Singh over at Bharat. Mina is here, but she's in the middle of something. I wanted to ask, what does she usually order from Starbucks?"

Chapter Nine

MINA DIDN'T KNOW how much longer she could hold out against Hem. She spent the week turning down his Starbucks lattes while eagerly waiting for their next meeting so she could spend more time with him. The emotional pull was exhausting, and when she woke up on Saturday, her thoughts were as fragmented as her feelings.

She sat on her plush couch, looking through a window of her small condo at a sliver of New York sky while she cradled a cup of chai. Despite her perfect Saturday morning setup, which included her faded NYU Law shirt and glowing skin from a sleep mask the night before, she couldn't relax.

Maybe her restlessness wasn't because of Hem at all. She still hadn't found any indication of her uncle's meddling yet, and that was wearing on her, too. She had a long way to go before writing her final due diligence report regarding WTA's tender offer. Hopefully, she'd discover the truth about Sanjeev's mole before she finished.

"There has to be something I'm missing," she muttered. She looked around her condo, hoping to find a tool that could help her get organized. She'd cleaned her space top to bottom the night before to blow off steam from the week. She'd washed and pressed her laundry like she did every Thursday. Her fridge was stocked since she had her groceries delivered. Maybe she just needed something as simple as a walk.

She got up with every intention of going out for fresh air when her phone buzzed. She walked over to the kitchen counter to read the messages on her screen.

HEMDEEP SINGH: You up yet?

Like her mom used to say whenever a person called who she was thinking about in the moment, Hemdeep Singh had a long life. Who would've thought that the man causing her such confusion would be the same one texting her first thing in the morning?

MINA: I'm up. Why are you asking?
HEMDEEP SINGH: I'll tell you in person. Pick up the phone.

Mina looked at her cell, confused by the last message. When her intercom buzzed, her jaw dropped.

"What the hell?" She answered on the third ring. "George?"

"Ms. Kohli," George from the front desk said. "I have a Hemdeep Singh here for you. Would you like for me to send him up?"

"Uh." She looked around at her apartment and then down at the half-empty chai mug in her hand. Her adrenaline spiked. "Uh, yeah. Yeah, send him up."

She practically threw the receiver against the wall. She started running toward the hallway before she realized she was still holding her mug. She raced back to the kitchen counter and put down the mug before vaulting over furniture and racing to her bedroom closet. She needed a bra before anything else. She pulled one out of her dresser and struggled into it. She then ran to the bathroom and tied her hair up in a messy bun. The doorbell rang just as she finished.

She yanked opened the door to a delicious Hem with day-old scruff, dark jeans, and a thin black button down shirt. His hands were tucked in his pockets and he leaned against her doorjamb.

"Morning."

"Damn it, Hem."

He leaned forward and gently pressed a kiss against her pouting mouth. She sighed under the soft brush of his lips and the sharp scent of woodsy soap. So she hadn't imagined his kisses from the previous weekend.

"I have been waiting to do that for days," he said.

Mina backed away and opened her door wider so that he could come in. He was too persistent to go away without a debate, and she had to admit she was curious as to why he was at her door. "It's Saturday."

"So I've heard." He kicked off his loafers and began a slow perusal of her place. "This is really nice. It looks like you. Elegant and vibrant all at the same time."

"I'm so glad I have your approval."

"Oh don't be like that," he said when he stepped into her kitchen. He looked at her mug, and after smelling it, he took a sip. "I'll make you more chai if you need more time getting ready."

"Where are we going?"

"On a date. I'm taking you out. You know, so we can get to know each other. Beyond the brief meetings and the one-time drunken whiskey night at a club."

"I thought we were going to keep it professional in the office."

He moved closer to her, and Mina tensed, as if his presence in her space was enough to spark the arousal. "Like you said, it's Saturday. We're not in the office."

"This is a bad idea."

He leaned into her touch, closing the distance between them. "I think it's a great idea. We're going to get brunch and then go to the planetarium."

"The . . . Wait, what?"

He dropped a kiss on the tip of her nose. "Just because I haven't brought up our debate about dating doesn't mean I've forgotten your point of view on how we need to keep away from each other. Hurry up, hiriye. We have planets to see."

She didn't know why, but after a few more moments of staring, she went to take a shower. Twenty minutes later she was dressed in a maxi dress with a matching cardigan. Her hair hung loose around her shoulders, and she wore ankle boots that were comfortable enough for walking. Instead of wearing a full face of makeup like she usually chose to do for work, Mina kept it simple with eyeliner, mascara, and lipstick.

"I'm ready," she said, looping her cross-body bag over one shoulder.

Hem held out one of her portable tumblers. "I made more chai as promised."

"Thanks, bab—I, uh, I mean, Hem."

His gaze darkened, and her stomach fluttered under his stare.

"Go ahead. Call me your baby."

"It's soon, Hem."

"And look at that. You haven't forgotten our dating debate, either. Honestly, it's not fast enough if you ask me. It's easy with you. Instead of fighting it, how about going with it just for today? See how it feels? This is uncharted territory for me, too, but I won't lie. I want this. I want you."

With a sigh, Mina took the tumbler. She wasn't one for lying, either. "Where are we having brunch?"

"Dosa Hutt."

"Really?"

"Really."

Hem led her down to his car, which he'd parked in front of the building. He slipped a few large bills in the doorman's fist before opening her door and then getting behind the wheel.

"So," he began. "NYU Law, huh?"

"Let me guess. Harvard?"

"Columbia, actually. I wanted to stay in the city."

"Makes sense to me."

They talked about their history, and how they survived the first few years out of school. Mina was so surprised to find the number of similarities they shared. Movies to live music. International travel destinations to weekend hot spots. Hem even described his last trip to Manila, and Mina couldn't help but salivate over the opportunity to engage in cutthroat contract negotiations overseas.

They crossed over into Flushing, Queens, faster than she could've imagined, and Mina watched in surprise as Hem navigated through the borough with deft familiarity. He parked in a small lot off Bowne Street and held her hand as they walked to the restaurant. It was a small hole-in-the-wall with cheap wobbling tables and random decor. The scent, however, was mind-numbingly delicious. Spicy and rich all at the same time.

They went to the back of the restaurant and ordered paper dosas, sambaar, and coconut chutney at the counter and then sat at a small table in the corner.

"This is nice," Mina said. "It's not every day I get to eat South Indian food with a North Indian man. A Singh brother no less. I wonder if anyone knows that your watch is worth more than most mortgages in this area."

Hem rolled his eyes. "Like my family's butler likes to say, don't obsess over appearances. Good food is good food."

Mina burst out laughing. It was only natural for her to reach out and lace her fingers with his. "Seriously though, do you take all the girls here to seduce them?"

"Nope. You're the first person I've ever brought to Queens. I was going to take you to Moghul Express, but that would've been too obvious. I figured you may like this better." He tugged on her hand until she leaned in. "You want to know something?"

"Always."

"My parents lived in Flushing before my father sold his first few patents. They used to bring me and my brothers here when we were kids. We loved my mom's cooking, but there was something special about cracking a two-foot-long dosa shell and dipping the fragments into a curried soup."

Mina smiled at the memory. She could almost picture them as children: Hem with his charm, Ajay with his seriousness, and Zail with his soft heart. "So why bring me here?"

"My father used to say that the best memories he had were of talking to my mom about his dreams and ideas right here in this restaurant. Mom would never tell him that he wanted the impossible. I want to share that with you today, Mina. Nothing is impossible. Not between us anyway."

She let out a sigh and tried to pull her hand away, but he tightened his grip.

"Talk to me. Please?"

She felt like he was cracking her heart open, and she wasn't used to being so vulnerable. The speed with which her control was unraveling scared her.

"I'm not used to this, Hem. I go on dates every once in a while just so I don't fall into a routine, but I don't *date*. I think I had one serious relationship in college that I knew wasn't going anywhere. I always put my career goals first. Men were too much of a distraction."

"Am I distracting you from your work?"

This time, she did pull away. "Actually, yes. Yes, you are."

"Is it worth it?"

"I haven't decided yet, honestly. We were supposed to take things slow and get to know each other while remaining professional. Isn't that what you promised me? The way you always look at me isn't professional."

"I could say the same."

"I mean it, Hem," she said. "This job is important. It's my mother's legacy, and I—"

She was interrupted when two trays stacked with disposable plates and long, spiral-shaped dosas were placed in front of them. *Thank god*, she thought. She was on the verge of telling him everything, and she wasn't sure if she was ready for that. Mina surveyed the food, aware that Hem didn't look away from her as he thanked the waiter.

"Well?"

"Well, what?" she said when she poked at her dosa to flatten it.

"Don't change the subject, Mina. You're not a coward."

She huffed out a breath. "And don't interrogate me, counselor. I'm not on the stand. Also, why is this about me? What about you? Didn't you just get out of a long-term relationship? According to my sources, you were almost at the altar."

Hem dipped a triangle of dosa into his sambaar and then coconut chutney. Mina watched him chew, his perfect mouth pressed together until he swallowed. His chest expanded with a deep breath.

"Lisa and I broke things off over a year and a half ago. And yes, I was hoping to propose, but it didn't get that far."

"What happened?"

"Lisa and I met in school and we kept in touch after we graduated. We ran into each other at a client's party a while back and a few dates after that, we slid into this easy companionship. Relationship," he corrected.

Mina continued to eat, waiting for him to tell her the rest.

"Besides a basic attraction, I think we started dating because we had similar career ambitions. She understood where I was headed at my father's company, and challenged me to always do more. To always want more. I don't know if she ever truly understood *me*, though."

"What makes you say that?"

Hem wiped his hands on a napkin before pushing up one sleeve to reveal a tanned forearm. His kara clanged against the table. "My father gave each of us our karas when we turned twenty-one. Lisa was fascinated by it since I wore it every day, all day and night."

"Yeah, well, it's your commitment to god and to your faith so why shouldn't you?"

His face lit up. "Exactly. She understood when I told her what it meant to me, but she couldn't comprehend how someone who was as educated, as wealthy, would still be connected to god. To her, religion was for the poor, and the desperate. No matter how many conversations we had, she still didn't get it. She wouldn't have understood this place, either. Lisa may have challenged my dreams, but she didn't necessarily support them."

Mina remembered the comment he'd made when they'd been in his apartment last weekend about Lisa's aversion to a T-shirt as a gift. "What about the clothes thing?"

"Pet peeve, I guess. It used to drive me nuts that I couldn't buy things for her to wear. Jewelry. Clothes. Anything. I loved the idea of seeing her enjoy something that I gave her, something that would make her feel as pretty as I thought she was. Instead, she refused to wear or accept anything I gave her except for the occasional birthday gift. A person is allowed to have boundaries. That wasn't the part that bothered me so much. It's why she had those boundaries in the first place. She said that it's better if our relationship wasn't on display. I never truly understood why she cared so much if people knew we were dating. The pride in me assumed she was embarrassed to be seen with a Sikh man."

Yikes. If Mina was dating someone, she'd want everyone to know how happy she was. As for the gifts, Hem was right. A person could have boundaries, and as long as she wasn't obligated to wear anything a man bought her, she'd be happy with whatever present she received.

"You had so many differences, yet you still wanted to marry her?"

Hem shrugged. "My parents were partners first before they grew to love each other. I figured that's what Lisa and I would have. We already loved each other, so we'd work out our differences with time. After two years, I introduced her to my parents, and well, they couldn't wait for my ex to make up her mind, so they pushed for a wedding."

Mina finished her dosa and tossed her napkin on top of her plate. "Wait. What do you mean when you say that they pushed for a wedding?"

"You know. They saw her, assumed that since I'd dated her so long that we were basically telling them we were going to get married. They started telling their friends that a wedding was coming up. They sent us information about banquet halls and wedding planners. Even when I told them to stop, they kept pushing and pushing. They freaked Lisa out."

"They're Indian parents, Hem. You should've known better than to introduce your girlfriend to them if you weren't one hundred percent sure that you were getting married."

Hem stayed quiet for a long time. A waiter came and cleared their plates away. "There were more issues with my family than just Lisa," he finally said. "This was around the same time that my father and some of Bharat's investors wanted the company to go public, which I was vehemently against. My father and I fought. Then Lisa and I started fighting. I thought it was a good time to strike out on my own, but she thought I was making the wrong decision when I voted against the family. In the end, she didn't support me, my future ambitions, and a future with us together."

"Oh, Hem. That's a lot."

"Let's just say that I handed in my resignation at Bharat the same day that Lisa told me that we were over."

Mina wanted to comfort him, to circle the table and crawl into his lap. He looked so reserved, so calm, but Mina could tell that he still hurt over the rejection.

Then it clicked. Her confusion that she was wrestling with that morning finally made sense. She looked around at the bustling restaurant, and then to the man across from her leaning back in his chair. It was a strange place to have a revelation about her feelings, honestly.

Hem was most definitely going to be a part of her life, either as a chapter or something more. She'd have to think about that and make sure she prioritized work at Bharat first to avoid an even bigger conflict of interest, but she'd worry about that later. Not here, not in a place that had so much history for Hem.

"Come on," she said. She stood and grabbed her purse. "Let's wash our hands and then get back to Manhattan. I'm ready to see some planets."

He looked at her warily before rising to his feet, too. "Okay, if you're ready to go."

"I'm ready," she said.

They went to the bathrooms to clean up first, and met at the front entrance. When they stepped out onto the sidewalk, Mina grabbed Hem's hand so they could both look up at the restaurant name painted across the awning.

"You know," Mina said, "I kind of understand why your father remembers this as where your mom believed in his dreams."

"Oh yeah? Why do you say that?"

"Because, Hemdeep Singh. While we were in there, it was so easy for me to believe in your dreams, too. For the record, anyone who knows you would've put their money behind your aspiration of opening up your own firm. It's going to undoubtably be a success."

The shadows in his expression faded, and Hem

pulled her against his side. He brushed his fingertips on the underside of her chin until she looked up at him and pursed her lips for a quick kiss. They linked their fingers together, a habit that was becoming more and more comfortable for Mina, and started toward the car.

"I can't believe you kissed me," he said cheerfully.

"What? You kissed me."

"There are aunties who probably saw us. Are baap re. So shameless to kiss a sardar on a sidewalk like that. What will your father think?"

Mina was still laughing by the time they reached his car.

Chapter Ten

MINA KNEW THAT two weeks wasn't a long time in a due diligence review, but she was starting to get frustrated by the following Friday. She had yet to find anything on Sanjeev, while compiling evidence that Bharat was indeed worth the purchase price. She hadn't told Hem or his brothers that yet, but she'd have to soon. She knew that due diligence reviews could take months, even years sometimes, but WTA and the board had her on a deadline. Not to mention, she hated the limbo she was in with Hem because of their work.

She leaned her head back against the train seat and tried to push thoughts of work and Hem out of her head. It was so hard when one of the two made her giddy like a schoolgirl.

After their weekend date to Dosa Hutt and the planetarium, she was more aware of Hem, more cognizant of how they looked together to other people. Meanwhile, Hem acted the same as he always had with her. Every time she was in the office, he made a point to bring her a venti skinny vanilla latte with no foam the minute she walked through the front doors. She thanked him in Punjabi and even called him endearments in her mother's tongue.

His eyes always seemed to light up whenever he responded in kind. It was as if he was sharing a secret with her, a secret he'd never told anyone else. She'd rarely dated Indians, and never Punjabis, so the language connection created a deeper level of understanding that was . . . intimate. More intimate than she'd expected.

"This is Metropark. Next stop, Metuchen."

The New Jersey transit automated voice pushed her out of her trance, and she got up, laptop bag and tote in hand, to follow a small crowd onto the train platform and down the stairs. She approached one of the idling cabs and recited her father's address for the driver.

"Are you Indian, ma'am?" the sweet-looking older gentleman said. He had a thick accent, and a weathered wrinkled face that made her think of happy grandfathers. His smile was bright and cheerful as he peeked at her through the rearview mirror.

"Isn't everyone Indian in Edison?" she said.

The man howled in laughter as if he'd never heard the joke before. "Where in India are you from?"

"My father is from Delhi, my mother from Amritsar, I'm from New Jersey," she said, reciting the same answer she'd given most of her life.

"Punjabi!" he said with such enthusiasm that he practically bounced in his seat. "I love North Indian food, but you know, not good for my blood pressure. Do you speak Hindi?"

She thought of Hem again, and the way he called her *hiriye.*

"Mostly Punjabi."

She enjoyed the driver's happy chatter as a distraction from the evening that lay ahead. Her father wouldn't change his mind about hosting a small dinner party for what she assumed was a client that Sanjeev planned on acquiring. She had no idea why her presence was required, but since she hadn't seen her dad in some time, she decided to make an appearance.

The cab pulled into a circular driveway in front of a large colonial home. She paid the driver and slid out of the car with her things just as the front door opened.

"Daddy?"

Her father, tall and broad shouldered, closed the door behind him. He wore the same black suit Mina had seen him in countless times before whenever they passed each other in the halls at the firm.

"I wanted to see if you were wearing heels," he said. He eyed her shoes and scowled. "Mina, you'll have to change out of those."

"You know I always take my shoes off when I come in the house. It's not that big of a deal." She gave him an air-kiss on his cheek and turned to walk inside.

"No, you have to wear shoes through dinner," he said, stepping in front of her.

"What? In the house? We never wear shoes in the house."

"Our guests don't believe in that cultural practice."

"Cultural pr—I thought they were super traditional!"

Her father crossed his arms over his chest. "Apparently, they still like their shoes on despite their preponderance for tradition. It makes them feel more American."

"Oh my god, they're heathens. Why do we want them as new clients again?"

"Mina," he snapped.

She laughed and patted him on his arm before walking past him. "If this so-called wealthy family and you want shoes in the house, I'll wear them to make everyone feel comfortable. But no one, even you, will tell me what kind of shoes I can wear."

"Are you trying to embarrass them?"

"No, of course not. It is, of course, fun to watch grown adults feel inferior to a tall woman with Louboutins."

She strode inside, feeling a little dirty about not removing her heels. She followed the sounds of chatter into her father's living room in the back of the house.

There were five people in the living room. Her uncles Sanjeev and Kumar, Mr. and Mrs. Aulakh, and Virat Aulakh, the man that her uncles wanted her to marry to secure the immigration law firm acquisition.

It was all starting to make sense as to why they wouldn't tell her the names of the clients attending the dinner party.

Virat leaned against the fireplace, holding a wineglass. His hair was cut short and his chin was still weak. His white button-down shirt was tucked into khaki pants and brown loafers. When he smiled at her, that bright, hopeful grin, she looked at the other two guests in the room.

Mr. Aulakh was dressed identically while Virat's mom wore a bright floral blouse. Unlike the other smiling members of the party, she glared at Mina's heels.

Deal with it, woman.

"Hello, everyone," Mina said, trying to take the identity of the dinner party guests in stride." I apologize for my delay. The trains are always so unpredictable."

"You should've taken a car, Mina," Sanjeev said. "Then you could've enjoyed Virat's wonderful stories about his trip to South Africa."

"Oh?" She placed her things on an empty seat at the end of the couch. "I didn't know you'd be here, Virat. I hope I still have a chance to hear about your trip." Virat approached her and Mina had to bend her knees so that he could press a kiss to her cheek. She remembered the first time she stood next to Hem. It had felt right, unlike the awkwardness she currently had to endure.

"Wine, Mina?" her father asked.

"Yes, please," she said. "Whatever everyone else is drinking."

"I'm drinking seltzer," Mrs. Aulakh said. She stood, her lips pinched, as she motioned to the glass in her hands. Her hair was cut in a militant bob colored an unnatural black and didn't move an inch when she nodded.

The woman held her glass up a little higher, pointing to it. Mina almost groaned. Virat's mom was one of those. The surviving breed of aunties that demanded traditional gender roles and suppression. Thank god her mother had taught her the difference between choice and ignorance.

Mina's father cleared his throat to interrupt the silence.

"I'll still have the wine, Daddy. Thanks. I'm Mina Kohli, Mrs. Aulakh. We haven't met. I see Virat has your beautiful eyes."

She softened at that and leaned forward for Mina to air-kiss her cheek.

"And you must be Mr. Aulakh. I read your white paper on the moral ambiguity of revoking work visas for valid H-1B spouses. It's a pleasure to meet you."

"You as well, guddia. You as well. It's nice to meet the woman that may cost me the law firm that I've worked so hard to build."

She ignored the childish endearment of *doll*, took the wineglass her father passed her, and then froze. "Wait . . . I'm sorry, what did you say?"

"I said it's nice to meet you since your marriage to my son may cost me my firm!"

She looked over at Sanjeev, who smirked at her.

That son of a bitch. He knew she wasn't going to start a fight in public, so he chose to fuck with her here in her mother's old home.

Mina plastered a serene smile on her face. "Well, I hope you'll consider the merger regardless of any proposed . . . arrangement that my uncles have hinted toward. I've seen the projections, the numbers, and I've done the benchmarking myself. You'd profit heavily from the deal."

"And Mina knows profitability!" Kumar Uncle said as he stood, patting his belly. "She's working on a case right now that I know will prove to be very profitable."

"Kumar Mamu," Mina said, using the respectful term for her mother's brother. "We don't know that yet."

"I do." He grinned.

Her father's cook stepped into the entranceway. "Dinner is served in the dining room, family style."

Mina stepped aside and motioned for Virat and his parents to go first. She held Sanjeev back, and when everyone was out of earshot, she whirled to face him.

"What the hell is this?" she hissed.

Sanjeev crossed his arms over his chest. "This is a business meal."

"They still think I'm going to agree to marry Virat, Sanjeev. What games are you playing?"

"None at all," he said. His skin looked oily in the dim light, and she hated that he always reminded her of a snake.

"You said that this wasn't an option any longer if I'm working on Bharat."

"But you haven't delivered on Bharat yet," Sanjeev said. "I don't know what's taking so long."

"It's due diligence, not a game of tic-tac-toe. I have to go through all the steps for the board."

Sanjeev stepped around her and started toward the dining room. "Fine. But until I get the answer I want from Bharat, you're going to be an eligible match for Virat. I'm going to get my worth out of working with you, Mina. Otherwise what good are you?"

His words were like a blow to her ego. She'd worked her ass off her whole life, and for Sanjeev to minimize her like that was painful. Instead of engaging, she squared her shoulders and followed him into the dining room. Virat and his family were already seated at the polished mahogany table. It was obvious that the empty seat next to him was where she was expected to sit. He smiled when she lowered onto the satin cushion chair and picked up a bowl in front of her plate.

Mina served herself some of the potatoes and held the dish out for Virat to take. He looked at her with a puzzled expression.

"Don't you want some?" Mina asked.

"Uh, sure." He took the dish and began scooping the food onto his plate. He passed it on to his mother, who shot daggers at Mina before she served her husband first and then herself.

Ah. Well, that explains it, Mina thought.

She dug into the potato curry with relish. Ignoring the evil side-eye she was receiving from everyone. She'd almost managed to zone out when she heard a phone buzzing from the other room.

Everyone paused and checked their pockets and devices.

"It's mine," she said quietly. "Feel free to ignore it."

"No, it's okay," Virat said. "I wouldn't be able to concentrate for the rest of dinner if I didn't see who called."

Desperately taking the opportunity for a few moments away, she mumbled an excuse and went back into the empty living room. Pulling her phone from the front pocket of her bag, she saw the missed call. Without thinking twice, she redialed.

"Hiriye," Hem said smoothly.

"Hem," she replied, with almost desperate relief.

"Mina? What's wrong? Are you okay?"

"I'm—I'm fine. Dinner at my father's house with some guests. It's a bit too much sometimes."

"In Edison?"

"How did you know that?"

"Background check. It's required for all consultants who are working on premises for extended periods of time."

"You could've told me."

"I figured you'd assume."

Mina let out a sigh and pinched the bridge of her

nose. "Hem, you looked into my life. I thought we were past the games."

"It's not a game. It was a formality. I'm sorry, though. You're right, I should've told you. Now are you going to tell me what's wrong?"

"Nothing, I . . . It's this dinner party. My father and my uncles are too much sometimes." She sat on the arm of the sofa and toed off her shoes. "I think I'm here for another hour unfortunately. Then I have to take the train back to Manhattan."

"Sit tight. I'll pick you up."

"What? Hem, you can't come here."

"I can. I'm in Alpine visiting my folks. It'll take me an hour with traffic this time of night, but that works with when you wanted to leave anyway."

"No, I'm fine. Please don't—"

"Too late," he said. "Mai tuhade lai a ri aahn."

I'm coming for you.

He hung up the phone with the type of finality that had Mina wanting and wishing their circumstances were different so she didn't have to take it slow.

"Mina?"

She jerked and almost fell off the arm of the couch.

Virat stood behind her, hands in his pockets. "Everything okay?"

"Yeah, everything's fine. I was . . . arranging someone to come and take me back to the city tonight. They were, uh, calling to confirm."

He nodded. Silence stretched between them for an

awkward beat. "Uh, I know we're in the middle of dinner, but I wanted to ask you if you'd be interested in going out sometime. We don't have to think about mergers and our family pressuring us into an arrangement. It'll be just you and me."

"Virat, I'm working on a really demanding case right now, and I really don't appreciate the family pressure that's coming along with the merger. I'm sorry. I just don't think it's a good idea for us to . . . You know what? How about we talk about this some other time?" She wanted to have a conversation with her uncle first before she told Virat that she had no intentions of agreeing to an arranged match.

Virat nodded, then crooked his elbow for Mina. She accepted his arm and walked with him barefoot back to the dining room.

"I have to say, I like you without the heels. I feel more comfortable when you're closer to my height," he said with a laugh.

"That's too bad. I always wear heels."

"Oh." Virat frowned.

She ignored his disappointment and slipped back in her seat after they reentered the dining room. "I apologize for the interruption, everyone."

"No apologies needed," Virat's father replied.

The conversation continued around Mina as she picked through her food, no longer hungry. She didn't know if it was because of Virat's comments on her heels, or because she knew she was about to see Hem again.

Forty-five minutes later, dessert was served and Mina helped pass around the bowls filled with sweet gulab jamun soaking in sugar syrup. She loved gulab jamun, but tonight, all she could do was push her dessert around in her bowl.

"Mina, do you cook?" Virat's mother asked, interrupting her thought process like a wrecking ball. The woman leaned forward and frowned at Mina's plate.

"I can cook, yes, though I don't have much time for it."

"Mina is an amazing cook," her father said. "Just like her mother used to be."

The praise would've meant something to Mina if it had been genuine. The truth was that her father had never had her cooking before. It wasn't until she'd started law school that she learned. Before then, her father had always had someone leave meals for her in the house.

"Mina, are you a lawyer because of your father and uncles or because of your mother?" Virat's father asked.

"My mother. She began Kohli and Associates."

"Yes," Sanjeev said with a sigh. "My sister was the oldest, and although she didn't have a good head on her shoulders, she managed to make a living."

Mina's fork dropped to her plate. The clatter was loud enough for the room to grow silent. "Mom was brilliant," she said. "She made sure her two younger brothers finished college and law school. She had a win rate better than her peers at a time when South Asian women were hardly allowed in the courtroom. She made a fortune before I turned ten. If it wasn't for her, none of us would be here."

Kumar snorted. "And if it wasn't for her, we'd already be a top ten firm. Her drinking problem got so bad that we were hemorrhaging clients. We almost had to sink the firm at one point."

"Not to mention, her late-night parties gave us such a bad reputation," Sanjeev added with a laugh.

"My mother didn't have a drinking problem," Mina said, gripping the edge of the table. The mere thought that someone would suggest it had her stomach churning.

Her heart pounded at the looks of pity from around the table. She expected her father to say something, to say anything, but he wouldn't meet her eyes. In the fifteen years since her mother's death, not once had anyone mentioned alcohol abuse.

"Mina doesn't see her mother the same way we do," Sanjeev said, his expression smug. "You didn't know about the drinking problem, did you? Nakhul, I'm surprised you kept that little gem from your daughter for so long!"

Kumar laughed. "Probably because he had to deal with Mina on a regular basis. Who wants to put up with our little Mina's fury?"

"I don't believe you two," she said, pointing to her uncles. "I knew her. And seriously, Dad? You're not going to say one thing to defend your wife?"

Virat's mother gasped. "You'd speak to your uncles and father like that?"

"Yes. And my mother did, too." Mina had had enough. She stood from the table for the second time during the meal, her hands shaking. "I just wish she learned earlier not to trust any of them. Excuse me, my ride should be here. It was a . . . pleasure."

She left the room, her strides stiff, her pulse fast. It took her three tries before she was able to put her feet in her shoes and grab her purse. She'd wait outside or at the corner of the block if she had to, but there was no way she could sit in that room with her family any longer. How dare they try to stain her mother's legacy? True, she'd been drinking the night of the accident, but that was the only time she'd gotten drunk . . . wasn't it?

Her uncles were full of bullshit. She had to find out what Sanjeev was doing with Bharat and hold him accountable. Then maybe she could kick him out of the firm, and she'd have a fighting chance of taking it over. She needed to honor her mother's legacy and she was ready to do whatever she needed to make it happen.

Her phone buzzed in her bag just as she reached the front entrance. She heard Virat call after her but she bolted outside and was already jogging down the walkway. Thank god for small miracles, she thought. The Tesla hadn't even come to a full stop when she yanked open the door and slid in the passenger seat.

"Mina? What—"

"Drive," she said.

Thankfully, Hem didn't argue. She saw Virat through the side mirror just as the car peeled onto the street.

Hem's warm hand touched her fist and stroked the tightness in her knuckles. The pressure was so soft, so comforting that she began shaking. Minutes passed, until finally Mina's grip loosened and she linked her fingers with Hem's.

Chapter Eleven

MINA STAYED QUIET until Hem drove into the mouth of the Lincoln Tunnel.

"Are you taking me to my condo?"

"No," Hem replied.

He'd braced himself for an argument, for some sort of reminder about her independence and how they worked together. Instead, she sank back into her seat in silence for the rest of the drive. He understood the importance of being alone, but he wasn't going to stand by without trying to take that haunted look off her face. After the weeks they'd spent together, circling each other, Hem knew that Mina was going to be his, damn it, and he'd protect her, even if he didn't know what he was up against.

It didn't help his mood that he'd just had an argument with his father. It was the first time Deepak

Singh had been well enough to come downstairs for a meal, and he and Hem had ruined his mother's dinner plans by picking at each other over business decisions, over Lisa, and the future of the company that he was no longer a part of. That he didn't want to be a part of. Focusing on Mina was a much better use of his time.

He worked through the possibilities of what could have made her so upset as he pulled into his building's underground garage and passed the keys to the valet.

Mina didn't argue when he took her laptop bag and led her into the private elevator and upstairs to his floor. When the doors opened, the New York skyline glittered through the windows and stretched to the horizon.

Hem kicked off his shoes and walked over to the com panel to turn on the recessed lighting to a dim glow. Mina slipped out of her heels and let out a sigh.

"Want some wine?" he asked.

"Yes, please."

"Any particular preference?"

"Surprise me."

He walked over to the wine fridge and pulled out one of his family's labels. "Why don't you get comfortable while I pour this for us? Your things are still in the master bath."

She turned away from the view and looked at him with puzzlement. "My things? What things?"

"The ones Rafael purchased for you a few weeks ago.

Also, I texted him when we hit that traffic on 95. I asked him to drop off more clothes. Some variety this time. They should be on the bed already."

"Hem, I'm going home tonight."

"That's your choice. But do you really want to sit around in the same work clothes you've had on since six this morning?"

"I'm dressed fine for one drink."

He grinned at her mutinous expression. "I like buying things for you. Well, I like whatever Rafael buys for you, knowing that I'm the one who gave them to you."

"Hem!"

"Please? I like it if you have things here. It makes me think that we're moving forward even though we're stuck because we work together right now."

Her expression softened. She walked over to him and stood on her toes to press a kiss against his cheek. The tension in his shoulders eased.

"I'll go look," she said quietly. "Only because I know it means a lot to you to do this. But if I don't like them, I'm not going to wear them. And I still may go home tonight. Understood?"

"Yes. Of course. I just want to make you happy."

Hem stifled a laugh at the way she turned on her heels and strode down the hall toward the master suite. If he had it his way, she'd be in his space, in his room all the time. She looked like she belonged here. His need for her grew with every long conversation at the office, every teasing text message, and every secret date. He knew he was ruined for other women; at least until his and Mina's time was up. And when she left him, he'd have to brace himself for a pain that would be so much fiercer than he'd ever felt before.

He'd finished pouring two glasses of Riesling when he heard the sound of the shower from the master bath. He left the glasses on the counter and headed toward the back of the penthouse to make sure Mina had everything she needed.

The bathroom door was closed, but there were multiple outfits laid out carefully on the bed with a discarded bag on the floor. Leggings, a thin jersey sweater, dark jeans, and a high neck sleeveless top with subtly sexy lingerie.

So she liked the clothes after all, he mused.

Since she was going to be comfortable, he might as well be, too. Hem took off his tie, button-down shirt, and slacks in favor of a pair of athletic shorts and T-shirt.

The shower shut off just as he returned to the kitchen. Five minutes later, Mina joined him in the great room, barefaced, her hair on top of her head, and dressed in the leggings and jersey sweater. She looked younger, more carefree, like she had the morning he'd showed up at her door, eager to see her again.

"I know this was a point of contention with . . . with your ex ," Mina said as she sat next to him on the couch. "So I won't push back on it, but don't assume you have other rights if I'm wearing the clothes you purchased."

"And get my balls chopped off? Never."

"I'm glad you understand. Now. I appreciate the clothes. Honestly, they're exactly what I needed."

He reached out to run a finger along the see-through mesh panel that stretched from mid-thigh to ankle. "I like this."

"Mmm-hmm." She took a sip from her glass, her eyebrows lifting almost to her hairline. "The wine is really good, Hem. What is it?"

"It's from our family's winery. Saffron Fields. The Riesling. I figured you'd like it."

"Saffron Fields is yours? No wonder it tasted familiar. This is like a hundred dollars a bottle. Is that part of Bharat, Inc.?"

Hem shook his head, distracted by the way some of her curls escaped the topknot and rested against her slender nape. "Saffron, along with our other ancillary businesses, are under Haz Industries. My father diversified after we were all born and decided to keep that part of his work separate from Bharat. Smart move on his part."

"Very," Mina mumbled behind her wineglass.

Hem grinned as he put his glass on the coffee table. He tossed one of the throw pillows at her legs, and before she could move, he lay down so his head rested in her lap. He expected her to push him away, but she began stroking her fingers through his hair. The feeling of her fingertips against his scalp sent sparks of sensation through his skin. He groaned and closed his eyes, enjoying the feel of her, the fresh floral scent on her skin.

"Hem?"

"Mmm-hmm?"

"Bharat has a little over a thousand employees, a location in California, London, Canada, and New York, and operates in a niche industry. And Saffron Fields has a great reputation, but it's not a large-scale operation. How has your father made it to the billionaire list two years in a row with a few, albeit successful, operations?"

Hem took her wineglass from her hand and put it next to his. Curling his fingers around the back of her neck, he pulled her down for a kiss so achingly sweet that he had to control himself from taking more. She tasted better each time.

Mina pushed against his chest and he reluctantly let her go.

"Hem," she whispered.

"Yeah. We have a sizeable agricultural business outside Vancouver managed by my mother's brother and wife," he said, pressing a kiss to her wrist. "Then there are the luxury high-rises in LA, Miami, Toronto, the hotels on Ibiza and the Amalfi Coast, and the shipping business in Mumbai. We have people we trust on-site to manage all of our extended property interests, but Ajay pulls the strings for most of it."

"You have other income streams. Why is it such a big deal if WTA buys out Bharat?"

"Because Bharat represents more to my father than a software company. It's his American dream. When his brothers and cousins were playing with toy guns and pretending to be cops, he was writing code. His greatest achievement in this world is something he wants to pass to his children, and we'll do whatever it takes to help him with that goal."

Mina brushed her fingertips against the diamond stud in his ear. "Family is important to you. You trust them to have your back when you need them the most."

"Yes."

"My mother trusted her family, too. It got her killed."

MINA KNEW THAT if something was going to happen between them, then she'd have to tell him the truth. She hated her history, but it was hers, so she'd tell it honestly.

"My grandparents on my mother's side died in a hate crime."

"God, Mina."

She gripped his fingers, holding onto them like a lifeline. "My mother had just graduated law school and ended up with two younger brothers in her care while grieving for the loss of her parents. She raised her siblings, though, while building a name for herself. She told me that my father didn't care that she was constantly worrying about her siblings. Her nurturing skills were attractive, apparently. They were both working for a top ten firm, and she'd just made partner when she got pregnant with me. She wanted a child of her own but knew that with her job, she'd just be an absentee mother."

"So she chose you over work?"

"Yeah, you can say that. She left to start her own firm. She was amazing, Hem. She ran a business, but I never felt neglected for a second. When we spent time together, she was one hundred percent focused on me. No distractions."

Hem sat up and pulled Mina onto his lap. The feeling was novel, and she enjoyed the rock-hard thighs under her, the supportive arm around her waist. She curled against him and tucked her head against his neck as she told him the rest. She mentioned the journals she found in the attic the day she moved the rest of her things out of the Edison house. She talked about the fight she had with her father and how he admitted that he and her uncles were celebrating the takeover of her mother's firm. She told him about Sanjeev's accusations over dinner and how her father didn't say anything at all to protect a woman he once had to have loved.

"That's why I'm determined to make partner," she said. "I'm going to take back Kohli and Associates and turn it into the firm that my mother always wanted it to be. We would've practiced side by side, you know. Instead, Sanjeev is at the helm, and god knows how he's managed to keep it a success."

"Hiriye," Hem said softly as he stroked her back from shoulders to hips. "I'm so sorry that you lost your mother like that, that your uncles are trying to ruin the precious memories you have of her. But I need you to think like the lawyer you are for a second. What was Sanjeev's motive?"

"What?" she asked. "What are you talking about?"

"If this was a dinner party, then why would they bring up such a sensitive topic in front of guests? Is there a reason why your uncle would say something like that in front of company? Airing family business doesn't seem his style."

Mina sat up. "I know. I know that Sanjeev is up to something like he always is. That he wants to prove a point. It's playing into this master plan of his that I'm a part of. I just have to figure it out."

"Are the guests part of the plan, too? The ones invited to dinner."

The roiling in her stomach grew stronger, and she got up from the couch and circled the coffee table to face him. "You could say that. Hem. Before I met you, there was . . . Well, let's just say that there's something else I have to tell you."

His expression darkened, but he braced his elbows on his knees and faced her. "I'm listening."

"My uncles have been trying to merge with an immigration law firm in New Jersey. The firm's owner is very traditional. His son Virat is single."

"No," Hem said. He shot to his feet, the words bursting from his mouth. "No, damn it."

"Sanjeev offered me equity partner if I went through with an arranged marriage to Virat Aulakh."

"You can't possibly believe they'll give you the partnership just like that. Look at how they screwed with you over dinner! Look how they screwed over your mother, and your mother raised them."

"Don't you think I know that?" Mina said. "I have no intention of marrying Virat, partnership or not. It wouldn't be fair to me . . . to—to us."

She saw him take a deep breath, and when he was about to step toward her, she held up a hand. "But all of this with my uncle has just made it all the clearer that we need to push the brakes until after the due diligence is over. I need to stop Sanjeev from destroying my mother's legacy, and what we have is just distracting me when my focus should be on work."

His face clouded with anger. "Like hell we're slowing down," he said, his voice controlled and low. He stepped over the coffee table and when he took her in his arms, Mina went willingly.

"Do you think we can stop this now?" he whispered as his mouth hovered over hers. "Do you want to?" She'd barely managed to shake her head before she was consumed with need. His kiss was fierce and all-consuming like a fire that swept over her. Her fingers dove into his hair as their mouths fused together. Mina's thoughts splintered and she gave into the overwhelming sensation of being devoured whole.

She didn't know when the kiss turned gentle, nor did she recognize the soft sob of passion that erupted from her throat. Hem pulled away, degree by slow degree, as his hands ran up her back and pressed against the sides of her breasts.

"Tell me you don't want more," he whispered against her lips, sipping from them, teasing her with the tip of his tongue. "Tell me you don't want this."

"Hem, you know I do, but we work together right now. We can't—"

"I told you," he said. "I'll wait to show the world that we're in a relationship until you're ready, but this won't work for me if you're going to cut me off at the knees and refuse to even acknowledge there is something between us."

Mina remembered his comment about how Lisa hid their relationship, and she wanted to soothe him, to give him everything he wanted just so he wasn't faced with old insecurities because of her. But their situation was different, and they had to be careful about different reasons.

He kissed her again, this time desperate and needy. She wrapped her arms around his neck and pressed against him, wishing things were different, hating that they had his father's work between them. Hating Sanjeev for complicating the one relationship she never knew she wanted. Then Mina stopped thinking all together and groaned into the kiss as Hem's grip in her hair tightened, as he pressed her impossibly closer.

She protested when he finally tore his mouth from hers, dragging in a deep ragged breath when Hem lifted her in his arms as if she weighed nothing. She was flat on her back on the couch a moment later with Hem coming down to lie on top of her. The jersey sweater was pushed over her breasts and he pulled down the delicate lace cups of her new bra until her nipples popped free.

Her sex clenched with need when he began sucking and caressing her breasts like a starving madman. She whimpered and rolled her hips, wanting more, mind-less with need for him. The leggings were yanked off her hips and she felt the cool air hit her thighs just as Hem pushed her legs apart and pressed a kiss to her navel, then to the apex of her thighs.

"Hem," she panted. She pushed her hips forward, wanting him to taste her, wanting the feel of his hot tongue touching her clit, wanting him to make her come in a way that she'd never experienced before.

"Mine," he said, then firmly licked the length of her pussy. With one hand he pressed his thumb against her clit, shooting sharp needlepoints of pleasure through her body.

Mina gasped and all the air pushed from her lungs as he pushed her legs farther apart and devoured her. He touched her clit with firm strokes and then pushed two fingers in her hard, jerking them fast and deep.

Mina didn't have time to prepare for the avalanche of sensation that rushed toward her. She plucked her nipples, panting his name, and screamed as Hem's fingers plunged deep and then curled to hit her G-spot. The orgasm rushed through her and she arched, suspended in that moment, quivering with desire and the feeling of Hem inside her.

Hem rested his forehead against her stomach. The room filled with heavy breathing and silence as Mina began to pull away, distinctly aware that his fingers were still buried inside her.

"Hem," she whispered.

He pulled out, and she felt the slick wetness between her thighs. She reached to adjust her clothes and was grateful when Hem stood and helped her to her feet.

Mina knew that it was natural, and she wasn't a stranger to sex, but she'd never met a man who enjoyed oral, who offered it so freely. Everything with Hem had been a first, and she knew in her heart, in her gut, that they'd hit another turning point. There was no going back now.

She grabbed her leggings. "I'll just be a moment," she murmured and rushed to the bathroom. She made quick work of cleaning herself up.

She felt a little bit more composed when she returned to the living room. Hem held out her glass of wine.

"Are you okay?" he asked, running a hand over her disheveled hair.

"Yes. I'm . . . Oh, you're still—"

"It happens. Around you, more often than not. What I gave you was for my pleasure, too. I don't expect it in return."

"Hem, I don't . . . I don't know what to do, and I always know what to do. You're throwing me off my game."

"Haven't you figured this out by now? It's not a game anymore. We're in this together. And one thing is certain. You have to tell him no, Mina. Goddammit, look at us. You know it'll be good. Forget Sanjeev. Tell this Virat guy that he doesn't have a chance. Be with me."

With a sigh, she reached out and stroked his cheek, feeling comforted by Hem's evening stubble. The rough, prickly sensation grounded her.

"Even after what just happened between us, there is so much at stake I still have to consider."

"You can handle your uncle."

"No, Hem, that's not all of it. Let's think this through for a second from Bharat's perspective."

"Bharat? What do you mean?"

"If I recommend that the company stay in your father's hand, and anyone finds out we're dating, my decision can be challenged because of my relationship with you. Then you're going to have to start the whole process all over again. Not to mention, my reputation will be questioned. I can't be distracted right now. For that reason, we hide what we have and then pick up after this is all over."

Hem led her back to the couch and nudged her until

she sat next to him, her head resting on his shoulder. "I won't hurt my father's chance at saving the company. But, Mina, after tonight, do you really think I can stay away? Could you? Honestly."

Mina looked up at the sharp angle of his jaw. "I—I don't know. I know that it's important enough to try."

He pulled her closer against him and kissed the crown of her head before resting his chin in that spot. "Fine, then give me this weekend. Be with me for the next two days and we'll try to go back to avoiding each other after that. We can go for a walk in the park. Have brunch. Movies, drinks, whatever you want. Until we go back to work, we'll be together."

"Won't it be harder for us on Monday then?"

"Yes."

The finality in his voice had her giggling. "You're a sucker for punishment then."

"From you? Most definitely."

She cuddled into him, as close as she could get. "Why couldn't you have been a nice Punjabi doctor from a good family? Then there would've been no opportunity for our careers to cross."

"Because what would be the fun in that?" Hem said with a chuckle. "Soon. We'll get through all of this soon, and then you'll not only be in my bed but in my home."

Mina sighed. She wasn't worried so much about where she'd end up, but how she was going to get there. Something wasn't right with her due diligence preliminary report, and she still hadn't told Hem about her uncle's second offer. It wasn't the right time yet, though. And Virat. Damn it, she'd have to put an end to that charade quickly. All without getting distracted.

Hem dimmed the lights so they could see the skyline clearly through the wall of windows. His scent wrapped around her, and as she slowly began to relax, Mina let herself hope that things were going to end up okay.

Chapter Twelve

HEMDEEP SINGH WAS obeying Mina's wishes so well that her sexual frustration was through the roof.

For two weeks, he kept his distance, and only engaged when she caved and went to him after work hours. In secret, they cooked and ate dinner together while passionately arguing cases that he was considering for his firm. They jogged in the park whenever they could. Weekends were for brunches and relaxing in front of the TV. However, at work, they were the perfect example of professional colleagues. It drove Mina crazy.

Her new involvement with Hem was probably why it took her so long to notice the lack of text messages from Raj. She'd been neglecting her best friend. It took time, but she finally called Raj and asked to meet for lunch.

Knowing that her friend was going to grill her the minute they saw each other, Mina arrived at the trendy downtown Indian gastropub first. She ordered a mango lassi with pistachio brittle and relaxed against the plush royal blue booth. The gastropub was a new edition to the restaurant scene, and the atmosphere screamed 1970s India glamour. From the pendant lights to the copper dishes, there wasn't a single detail that hadn't been taken into account.

Mina was about to text Raj when she heard the whoosh of the front door. Her best friend stepped through the entrance and paused to scan the restaurant. Her elegant pose turned heads.

As always, Raj knew how to be fashionably late. Mina raised her hand and waved. "Right here!"

It wasn't until Raj came closer that Mina started to notice the outfit was all wrong. Instead of Manolos or Louboutins, Raj had swapped her glam heels for a pair of white sneakers. When she unbuttoned her trench coat, she revealed a white tailored button-down shirt tucked into a pair of dark blue jeans. A slim Chanel belt glinted at her waist.

"Hey," Mina said slowly.

"Hey." Raj handed her coat to the waiter, who hung it on a hook next to a teal antique mirror. "I wasn't at the office."

"Yeah, I was wondering about that. Everything okay?"

Raj sighed. "I've been with my attorneys for the last week. We're ... working on something that I don't want my husband to see."

"Oh? Is there anything I can help with? You know, as your attorney best friend."

"I wish. I'd trust you more than anything, but I don't want to put you in the middle."

Mina leaned forward and touched Raj's hand. It was devoid of the bloodred polish she was so fond of. "Raj, what's going on?"

"I can't tell you just yet." Her voice broke, and when she took off her sunglasses, Raj's eyes were framed with deep bruised bags. She looked like she hadn't slept in days. Her skin was also noticeably ashen under a mismatched shade of beige foundation.

"Oh, honey."

"I promise that when it's all done, you'll be the first person I'll celebrate with, but for now, it's better if I keep all the cards to myself."

Mina pushed her mango lassi forward. "I think you need this more than I do."

Raj didn't argue and took a healthy gulp from the glass. "Please distract me. Tell me about your sardar, and if he's as dominating in bed as I imagine."

Mina hesitated. She wanted to push, wanted to make sure Raj was okay, the same way Raj always checked up on her. It was so strange seeing her vibrant, capable friend looking haggard and . . . normal. "Raj, I'm here for you. Please talk to me."

Raj reached out again and gripped Mina's hand this time. Her fingers squeezed. "I promise everything is okay. I'm in the middle of a hasty . . . dispute. It's big and it'll affect my life in a significant way."

"Then let me help."

"I will. Not yet. Please."

Mina sighed but made a mental note to check in on Raj more often. "Fine. But I can't be distracted for long."

"Don't I know it," Raj said with a laugh. "Come on. How is he in bed?"

"Well, we haven't exactly been there yet."

Raj's eyebrow arched in a perfectly smooth lift that helped Mina relax. The waiter came at that moment, and they paused to order.

"Why haven't you taken advantage of him?" Raj asked when they were left alone again.

"Because we're trying to avoid any complications with his father's company. If I get involved with the owner's son, my decision can be challenged as not being impartial." Mina told Raj about the fight she'd had with her uncles during the dinner party, and the resulting weekend she spent with Hem. She even told her that she'd left most of her new clothes at his house, hanging in the empty closet of one of the guest rooms, because he wanted pieces of her there. She mentioned the stolen kisses over the last two weeks, and how it was getting increasingly difficult to look unaffected by his presence. Their food was served, and they continued to talk about Mina's predicament as they devoured their food.

"I still have to talk to Virat and my uncles about the merger," Mina said. "I wanted to do it right after I came back from Hem's two weeks ago, but I'm worried my uncle will retaliate. I feel like he's starting to realize how much time I'm spending on the Bharat project and I don't want him to pull me off that as punishment."

Raj tapped her lower lip as she finished chewing her pappadum coated in cheese fondue. "I'm still stuck on how Sanjeev knows so much about Bharat technology. I may be naturally suspicious of men, but that's where I would focus."

"I am. Or I was. I'm not coming up with any leads."

"Start looking in the unexpected places. You need to find out what Sanjeev wants more and dangle that in front of his face so he forgets the rest."

Mina nodded. "I'm meeting with Bharat's head of research and development today. She flew in from California."

"She?"

"Yes. Zail knew her at MIT. Since Sanjeev's lead has to do with new technology, I'm hoping that this director will lead me in the right direction."

Raj leaned back in her chair. She opened her mouth to speak when her phone buzzed next to her empty thali.

"Shit, yaar," she said. "Can I take this?"

"Yeah, of course."

Mina took a moment to pick up her phone and check her messages as well. She heard Raj mention something about a dissolution, but her attention was immediately diverted to the text from Hem.

> HEM: Are you coming into the office today?
> MINA: Yes. Finishing up lunch with Raj.

Mina began to exit out of her messenger app when Hem responded right away.

> HEM: Come home with me afterwards.

It was the first time he'd asked her to spend time with him outside the office. The text left her warm and tingling inside.

> MINA: I shouldn't.
> HEM: I want another weekend together. Just you and me. No, I need more than a weekend. This is driving me crazy.
> MINA: Me, too. Hem, you and I both know why we should wait.
> HEM: Dammit Mina, I want you until you scream. I want us sweaty and moaning in bed. I want to feel your heels pressing into my back as I taste you. And then I want to wake up next to you and watch the sunrise with you naked and warm beside me.
> MINA: After the quarterly board review. Then I'm yours.

HEM: That's too far away.

MINA: We'll suffer together.

"That must be a damn good text," Raj said. Mina looked up, surprised to see her friend smirking behind her glass.

"I'm in trouble," Mina replied. She let out a ragged breath as the truth of her words hit her like a semi. "Damn it, I'm in real trouble." She'd never felt the way that Hem made her feel. She'd never been sucked in with so much intensity. She wasn't sure how she was supposed to handle him or if she could handle him at all. They weren't even dating and she felt consumed.

"He's different, Mina. I can see it on your face. Do you want my company to do a discreet background check? It's not exactly ethical, but I can get you history on finances, any gambling issues, drinking issues, drugs, secret women, you name it."

Mina laughed. "I've spent enough time with him to know that Hem doesn't do secrets well."

"That kind of guy, huh?"

"Yes. I have to talk to my uncle soon. I need to take control of my life again."

Raj leaned forward and touched Mina's hand. "I know taking back your mother's company is important to you, but if they fire you, I know there are other things you can do to reclaim your mother's name."

Mina didn't want to think about that possibility. She was so close to getting where she needed to be. The idea of giving up now was too painful to imagine. "What would you do if you were in my position?"

"I would have fun," Raj said. She leaned back in her seat again, waving a hand toward the waiter for the check. "You and I have spent way too much time trying to prove to ourselves and others that we aren't like our family, that we aren't pawns on someone else's chess board."

Mina wished it was that easy. "What do you think I should tell my uncle?"

"To fuck off."

"Raj. Seriously."

"I am being serious, Mina. I'd tell your uncle to screw himself, and then go do other things. Then he'll have no control over you. The only reason he does is because you're allowing it."

"It's not that easy, damn it. I'm doing this for my mother."

"But what if this isn't what she would've wanted? What if your mother's hopes for your future were so much greater than hers? You're making assumptions here, Mina."

"I have to try it this way. If it doesn't work, then I'll do something else, but for right now, this is the best option for me."

Raj let out a sigh. "Fine. If you think so, then I'll support you."

"Thank you."

She followed Raj out of the restaurant and onto the

sidewalk. There was a distinct spring breeze that carried with it the smell of neighboring restaurants and street smog.

"Why can't life be simpler than it is?" Mina said.

Raj slipped the glasses back on her face. The corners of her mouth tightened as she said, "Because life isn't about simplicity or happiness. Sometimes, it's a straight-up fucking tragedy, and we have to deal with it."

The words were so harsh, so different than what Mina was used to, that she reached out and hugged Raj as tight as she could. Her friend shook for a moment, before returning the embrace.

"I'm giving you a couple weeks," Mina said. "Then I'm going to start harassing you on a daily basis to find out what's happening."

"I need a month and then I'll share everything."

"Promise?"

"Promise."

Mina watched as her friend slipped into the back of her private vehicle and drove away before calling a car to take her to Bharat's offices. Raj was never cagey, or secretive about projects she was working on. Whatever was happening was causing her a significant amount of pain.

She was so lost in thought that Mina jolted when her phone buzzed in her hand.

With a sigh, she answered. "Mina Kohli speaking."

"Hi, Mina, it's Virat Aulakh. How are you today?"

"Hi, Virat, how can I help you?"

"I was wondering if you'd be interested in meeting

with me for dinner tomorrow night? Six thirty? I'm in New York and I can meet you at a place close to your offices."

She mentally reviewed her calendar and the list of things she wanted to accomplish before the weekend. It wasn't as much as she'd expected, and even though she wanted to talk to Sanjeev first, it didn't hurt to speak with Virat about her situation.

"There's a restaurant in my building. I'll meet you outside."

"Wonderful," he said. His voice softened. "Looking forward to celebrating with you."

"Celebrating? Celebrate what?"

When silence greeted her, she realized that he'd already hung up the phone. Maybe he assumed that she'd accept his offer despite her noncommittal stance on the issue. When her car arrived, she slid into the back seat, irritated that she had to deal with him, too.

"Men," she muttered.

A moment later the driver's voice interrupted her thoughts.

"Mina, right? Great name. Where are you from?"

Chapter Thirteen

BY THE TIME Mina set up her workstation in a conference room at Bharat, she was forced to swallow a
couple Advil to stave off a headache. Between Raj,
Virat, Hem, and her uncles, she had more personal
issues than she cared to think about at once. She had
started her computer and logged into Bharat's network
when she was interrupted by a young woman holding
a venti Starbucks cup.

"Ms. Kohli?"

"Yes?"

"I'm Tiffany, Mr. Hemdeep's personal assistant. He
requested that you receive this today," she said. Tiffany
placed the cup in front of Mina and the fragrant smell
of vanilla wafted around her. She nearly groaned with
pleasure.

"Thanks." She was still swooning over Hem's thought-fulness when she realized what the woman had said. "Personal assistant? I didn't realize he had one."

"I just started," Tiffany replied. She straightened in her pressed black pantsuit. "I'm stationed at his law firm across town, but he wanted to make sure you were comfortable today."

She looked over one shoulder then the other before she whispered, "I'm supposed to wait until after work to ask, but for the sake of efficiency, Mr. Singh is hoping to add some things to his penthouse for you, and has requested that I get your list of preferred beauty products."

Mina almost choked on her latte. *"What?"*

Tiffany pulled out her phone, still whispering. "Would you like to speak with Mr. Singh? He said you wouldn't approve."

Wouldn't approve was putting it mildly. "Can you tell him that he can shove—"

"Tiffany, I think Rafael is looking for you," a voice said from the doorway. Mina looked up to see a beautiful pale face with large dark eyes framed in tortoiseshell glasses.

"Hey!" Tiffany's voice returned to its normal volume. "Thanks, Sahar. It's nice running into you again! Cute outfit." Tiffany turned back to Mina. "I'll get that information from you at a more convenient time, Ms. Kohli. Have a great day. Let me know if you need anything else."

Tiffany slipped out of the room as quickly as she'd

entered, leaving Mina with Sahar Ali Khan, Technical Director of Research and Development at Bharat, Inc.

"Tiffany has been buzzing in and out of the office for the last two days," Sahar said. "Rafael is supposed to teach her the ropes. She's eager to learn and she's smart, but sometimes she lacks subtlety."

"I can see that," Mina replied, motioning to her latte. She stood and offered a hand. "It's nice to finally meet you."

"Yeah, you, too," Sahar said as she took the hand. Her bones were slender and delicate compared to Mina's. Her grip, however, was just as strong.

"If you heard a word of what Tiffany was suggesting . . ."

Sahar shrugged and closed the door behind her. "I don't tell secrets," she said. "My lips are sealed."

"Thanks." Mina motioned to the chair next to her and waited until Sahar sat in it and folded her legs so that her white Converse were tucked under her knees. "You're normally in the California office, right?"

"Yup. Me and my team are there. I don't make it out to New York much because management comes to me. Zail is normally in Cali and we're blessed with Deepak Uncle's presence every once in a while, when he likes to tinker in the lab. He's still as sharp as a tack so we welcome his intrusion."

"Well, I appreciate you coming here for a debriefing. I know we were trying to get something set up for the first week I started on Bharat's due diligence report."

"Yes, sorry about that. There are a ton of clearances I had to go through before I could talk to you about our research. Since we finally filed our application, it's a little easier for me to get you up to speed. I'd like to go over our most recent project—I think it'll triple our revenue and hopefully make your life easier."

Mina raised an eyebrow and took another sip of her latte. It was obvious that Sahar was on Team Turn-down-the-offer. "I'm always up for making life easier, but I have to admit, you're the first employee who has even hinted at your feelings regarding WTA."

"I'm a Pakistani-American woman in the tech industry. Not many people respect and appreciate my skills. Deepak Uncle sought me out, offered to mentor me, and treats me like a professional. I know for a fact I'm not going to get that at WTA."

"Fair point," Mina said.

"May I?" Sahar said, motioning to the laptop.

"Sure."

She pulled it onto her lap and began typing. "The information I'm about to show you was only available to me and a team of six people until last week. I can't give you hardcopies of anything for confidentiality purposes, I'm going to lock you out your computer temporarily so I can give you a visual."

Mina nodded and watched as Sahar pulled a storage device from her pocket and plugged it in the USB port. She then folded the laptop back into a tablet and held it out for Mina to see.

"This is it," Sahar said with pride in her voice.

On the left side of the screen was a navigation bar, on the bottom was a compile box, and the top half of the pane was crammed with lines of Python code, some highlighted in neon colors, vividly displayed against a black screen.

"Uh, Sahar? I have some technical knowledge but you're going to have to actually explain to me what this software does."

"Oh," Sahar said, taking the tablet back. "Sorry. I guess I missed a few steps." She tapped the screen and started scrolling through the code, her eyes bright behind her glasses.

"It's deep learning technology. A type of intelligence that Bharat has created to help locate difficult to find objects. It can save lives, corporate and national revenue. To be more specific, this software can locate moving targets traveling at over two hundred miles an hour. The accuracy rate is over ninety—"

"Ninety-eight point eight seven percent," Mina finished. Her stomach knotted painfully, her throat drying at the realization of what Sahar was telling her.

"Y-yes," Sahar said. Her eyes went wide with shock. "How did you know that?"

Silence stretched between them and Mina looked into the other woman's face, horror growing in her gut. She recalled Sanjeev's words when he first spoke to her about Bharat, Inc. He'd told her about the software with almost the exact same description.

"Is it—is it used to find missing persons?"

Sahar nodded slowly. "We've already received some inquiries from the military after we filed our application. We think that the government wants to use the technology for missile location. That's not why we created it, and—"

"I need you to answer a question for me and I need you to keep it in this room," Mina said. She leaned forward, her elbows on her knees, and her sweating palms clasped together. "Did you share any of this with the board of directors?"

Sahar shook her head so hard that her ponytail whipped her in the face. "No. Like I said, my team of six knows about this. Oh, and of course Deepak Uncle, Zail, and Ajay. I don't even think Hem has an idea of what we're trying to accomplish. Mina, how do you know about my project?"

Son of a fucking bitch, Mina thought. She may not have found the mole, but she'd sure as hell found the right team. Usually it was Finance that leaked information, but she should've guessed R&D as the second choice. If she hadn't been so distracted, she would've made the connection. It didn't help that it had taken so long for Sahar to come out and meet with her.

What was done was done. The only problem Mina had now was that the information leak was so much bigger than she expected. Like national-security big.

She bolted to her feet, grabbed her phone, laptop and her purse, and strode toward the door. "We didn't have this conversation, okay? Your team doesn't know about it, no one."

Sahar's eyes had gone glassy with unshed tears. Her breath hitched but her voice was firm and as strong as her handshake. "How much more do you know, Mina? I have to figure out where to start damage control."

"Not much, but someone else might have more intel. You can't let on that you know. If you're loyal to Bharat, keep it as quiet as you can until the leak is found."

Sahar stood on quivering legs. "Two years. This took two years and countless sleepless nights, weekends, missed vacations. I have to tell the Singhs first and then I'm going to have to go back to California. If you need anything, you'll have to come out to see me. I—I can't leave again."

In the weeks that Mina had been at Bharat, she'd learned how passionate the Singhs were about their company. Deepak Singh didn't deserve to have his business destroyed by greed. She had to deal with this now. Today. "Let me tell the Singhs. I owe it to them. I'm sure Zail will talk to you tomorrow."

Sahar nodded as she pocketed the dongle that had brought up the software on Mina's machine. "I'm sorry our meeting got cut short."

"Me, too. Good luck." Mina knew that she was trusting Sahar at her own risk. The director was aware that Mina had made the connection to leaked information and her team. Sahar didn't seem like the type of person to engage in corporate espionage, but at this point, everyone was a suspect.

Mina bolted through the office. She saw Rafael's and Tiffany's startled expressions as she ran by them and straight into an open elevator. She was in a cab heading to Kohli and Associates in moments.

First stop was Sanjeev. She had enough information that she could confront him now, and try to force him out. How was she going to do it, though?

"Think, Mina, think," she said, pressing her fingertips to her temples. If her uncle was dealing with trade secrets, then every attorney at her mother's firm would be questioned, including herself. She could lead with that.

No, Sanjeev only ever worried about himself. She'd have to hurt him where it mattered the most.

Her mother's firm.

She got out of the car and took the elevator up to the office. Before she stepped through the glass doors, she paused and looked down at her phone. She needed to take extra precautions if she was going to confront her uncle about something that could land him in the middle of an FBI investigation. Mina turned on the recorder app.

When she was sure her phone was ready, she exited the elevator vestibule, badged into the office, and was greeted by the sounds of keyboards, conversation, and ringing phones. A few people waved to her as she walked down the hallway toward the partner offices.

Lies. All of this was built on lies.

Sangeeta, her uncle's secretary, looked up in surprise when Mina walked by her desk. "Mina? Your uncle is in a conference call. I can page you at your desk when he's done."

"That won't be necessary," Mina said and pushed open his door, phone held in one hand, purse in the other.

The room smelled of smoke and sweat. The windows were cracked and her uncle had someone on speaker as he leaned back in his leather chair, hands clasped on his bulging belly. There was a distinct yellow mustard stain on his shirt.

Sanjeev looked over at Mina, glaring before he said, "Gary, I'll call you back. I may have information for you sooner rather than later."

A man grunted on the other end of the line. "This is taking too long. Call me soon."

The lines disconnected.

"Mina, what are you doing here? Isn't today the day you're supposed to be at the Bharat offices? I want that case wrapped up."

Mina hated litigation for a reason. She had a very hard time controlling her emotions, and she knew she couldn't control the rage that vibrated in her voice. "Is that the person you're leaking information to?" she said.

She saw the surprise on Sanjeev's face before it was masked by his legendary poker face.

"You obviously came here to say something."

Mina put her purse on one of the chairs and sat in the other. She still held her phone in one hand and rested it on her knee.

"You've been negotiating for trade secrets that could affect national fucking security, Sanjeev."

"That's a hefty accusation from my niece," Sanjeev said. "I told you that there are certain things done in business that—"

"Do you remember what you told me the first day that we talked about Bharat? How I was supposed to do a due diligence report?"

The corner of Sanjeev's mouth twitched. "What are you getting at, Mina?"

"I want to revise the deal."

"Did we have one?"

"I'm not here to waste time."

"Oh?" He laughed, and the sound was as noxious as the smell in his office. "Well it appears that you're fine wasting my time."

Mina stood. "Right now it looks like Bharat will turn down the offer. Too bad for you."

"What?" He bolted up in his chair. "Damn it, Mina. Bharat needs to accept the offer."

"Why?"

"It's not your concern."

"It is when you know about a patent application that hasn't been released to anyone outside of the organization."

He waved his hand in dismissal. "Getting the information from Bharat's team was easy. Anyone can be bought with enough money. Half the board knows that they've been working on this software. It's going to make us a lot of money if WTA uses it for military intelligence."

"Who at WTA know this?"

"Why does that matter to you? You have one job, Mina. Nothing else is important."

She leaned forward, fury burning in her blood. "Listen up, old man. I know that you don't care if you've put everyone here at risk of losing a job and their careers. But if this gets out, you'll be spending all your money on making sure you don't go to prison. If you take an early retirement and leave the firm, you'll save jobs and time with the authorities."

Sanjeev burst out laughing. He pushed away from the desk and spun in his chair like a child who had heard the best thing in his life. "Leave the firm? What, to *you*? Mina, Kumar and I built this firm into the powerhouse it is today." His words sounded thick with an accent, and his English broke to reveal his Punjabi roots.

"*Muma* built this firm."

"Your mother was a drunk," he said, spittle projecting from his mouth. "She was controlling and manipulative, and I did what I had to do to beat her. Look at the empire I've created. You're only here because your father protects you."

"How dare you? She *raised* you, Sanjeev." Mina's voice shook.

"You, Mina Kohli, never saw the ugly side of that bitch. You're lucky that all you had were perfect memories and a few diaries."

"Those memories and diaries are more trustworthy than you are, you son of a bitch."

"That I am, but you're her spawn. Don't think for a second I don't see her filth in you every day. You won't have this firm as long as I'm alive." His fist pounded on the desk and every item on its surface shuddered from the impact.

Mina knew her mother, and she'd seen Sanjeev in action her whole life. He was wrong about her just like he'd always been wrong about Mina. She stood, chilled despite the temperature in the room.

"What makes you think," she said slowly, "that I haven't already won? With the way you've screwed with Bharat, you'll be in jail soon enough and your career will be as good as dead. Kumar's, too."

Sanjeev laughed again, this time with a hint of menace. "Little girl, I've been playing these games longer than you have. Why do you think I have you running due diligence? You're just another chess piece in my master plan."

Chess piece.

Master plan.

It all started falling in place. Shit. She'd been more distracted than she thought to miss something so glaringly obvious. "You told me about what decision you wanted so I'd look for the mole, didn't you? Once I was in close enough proximity to the mole, you would've filed a false claim that I was behind the info leaks. You'll make the connection between proximity and probable cause."

"Finally! She's figured something out."

"Then you'd pin all of this on me. You'd ruin my career, just like you ruined my mother's career?" She shoved back away from the desk, ashamed that she'd been stupid enough to not think beyond her own wants and needs as partner of her mother's firm. "You never intended to give me any partnership position."

"No, of course not. It's business, Mina. And you're disposable." He picked up his phone and motioned to her. "Now get out of my office. I was going to be gentle and just screw you out of a job, but if you vote against me on WTA's offer for Bharat, then I will destroy your future. Are we clear?"

Mina knew when it was time to pull back, and when it was time to charge. She picked up her purse and turned to leave.

"This isn't over, Sanjeev," she said and slammed his office door behind her.

She took a moment to close her eyes and let out a breath. Raj's words from lunch came back to her like a sorry reminder.

I know taking back your mother's company is important to you, but if they fire you, I know there are other things you can do to reclaim your mother's name.

"Ms. Kohli? Mina?" Sangeeta said from her desk.

Mina opened her eyes to look at Sanjeev's pale assistant. She'd obviously heard most of the conversation. Mina would be surprised if Sangeeta didn't hear most of Sanjeev's conversations. She looked down at her phone and up again.

"I'm—He's—Ms. Kohli."

"You worked for my mother first, Sangeeta, before you spent years watching Sanjeev ruin lives," she said quietly. "If you have anything on Sanjeev. Any emails. Save them and send them to me. I'd protect you for the help you'd give me." She turned to walk away, ignoring the rest of the curious faces in the office.

Once she was in the elevator, she checked the recording on her phone. The sound was low, but clear enough to hear every word. She then sent a quick message to Hem.

> MINA: Where are you?
> HEM: With my brothers. What's up?
> MINA: Need to see you.
> HEM: Is something wrong? At Ajay's.
> MINA: Yes. Address? Your brothers need to hear this, too. I can be there in an hour or two tops.

He sent a Google pin moments later.

> HEM: I'll be waiting for you, hiriye.

Chapter Fourteen

HEM CHECKED HIS watch again. Mina said it would take her an hour or two to get to the penthouse. It had been almost two hours, and he was running out of patience.

"She'll be here soon." Zail clapped Hem on the back before he picked up the cue chalk and tended to his pool stick.

"Are you going to tell her what we found out about her mother, bhai?" Ajay asked.

"In time." Hem still cringed when he recalled the details of the full dossier he received from investigators. He'd wanted the report because he wanted to understand Mina better. Now, he'd wished he'd left it alone.

"I think she's uncovered our mole," Zail asked.

Hem grunted as the sound of pool balls cracking

echoed through the room. He'd been brainstorming all day with Ajay and Zail, trying to figure out how Bharat was losing money when in truth, they should be making it.

They'd even conferenced in their father, taking a chance on the fact that the issue wasn't going to upset his health. Deepak didn't react the way they expected. Their proud, strong dad who'd built an empire and taken care of his family, looked defeated and pale. His wide shoulders slumped under the weight of the news Ajay delivered with diplomacy.

"The company I built, the people I took care of, have betrayed my heart," he said in gruff Punjabi. "I have failed my sons and the legacy I've left behind."

Before Hem could do or say anything to convince him to relax, he lost the connection. That was when he texted Mina in the afternoon. He knew she'd been out to lunch but connecting with her always helped him put things in perspective.

The doorbell rang and he nearly vaulted over the railing that sectioned off the gaming area from the rest of the room. Ajay beat Hem to the door, and when he opened it, Mina stood in the entrance with her hair pulled back in a French braid. She still wore the heels that she loved so much, but instead of a purse, she carried a large brown paper bag and a backpack.

"I bought takeout," she said. "Hopefully it's enough of a peace offering that you won't kick me out after I tell you what I know."

Ajay took the food from her and motioned her into the house. She looked around, eyes rounding at the expansive kitchen that took up most of the main floor. Ajay enjoyed cooking more than Hem and Zail, so he'd gone overboard in that section of his penthouse.

Mina kicked off her heels, dropped her pack, and headed straight for the windows that faced the East River. The view was different from Hem's place, but just as stunning.

"I need to get me one of these," she said, motioning to the two-story windows. "My condo is nothing compared to the digs that you rich munday have."

"Well, us Punjabi boys won't be rich for much longer if we don't figure out what's happening with our company," Ajay said as he began unpacking the food. "Where did you order from?"

"There's a Thai place near my apartment. I picked up a few options. Go ahead and eat whatever you want."

Hem couldn't wait to touch her any longer. He crossed to her, ignoring her startled expression, and wrapped his arms around her waist. Mina stiffened for a moment, before returning the embrace and leaning her head against his shoulder. The heat from her touch was the sweetest pleasure after such a long week.

"Shit day, huh?" he murmured in her hair. It smelled like kiwi and papaya, the same as the shampoo she'd left in his shower.

"You have no idea."

"Why don't you tell us about it?" Zail called out. He

started digging through the plastic takeout containers until he settled on one that looked like green curry with jasmine rice. Ajay handed him a set of chopsticks and a spoon.

"Out of all three of you, you're the first one who should sit down, Zail."

He froze. "I'm not going to like this, am I?"

"I don't think so."

Hem led Mina toward the table and nudged her into an empty chair. "Start from the beginning," he said.

"Okay, but first, before I tell you anything, I'm going to call in my favor."

"Your favor?" Ajay asked.

"Yes. The one you gave me when I agreed to keep your father's health a secret. No matter how you feel about me when I'm finished, I need your word that you'll help me find a way to hold Sanjeev accountable for what he's done."

"Agreed," Hem said. "I don't like that bastard."

"He has something to do with the shit that's happening at Bharat?" Zail asked as he combed his fingers through his thick beard.

"You have to realize that not only did I not know any of you, but I had no intention of helping my uncle with his plans for Bharat." Her voice was steady, strong even, with an underlying tone of anger, as she told them about the meeting she'd had with Sanjeev when she learned about her due diligence assignment.

"I had every intention of remaining unbiased," she said. "But I was going to find the mole and force Sanjeev out of his current position. Now I know that my uncle wanted me to be his scapegoat, and he planned on screwing me no matter what happened. Once I uncovered the mole, he'd frame me because I'd be the closest to the leak, and then run off with the money."

"You should've come to me, Mina," Hem snapped, anger boiling as he realized how close she was to the reasons behind his father's failing company. "We could've solved this sooner."

"Stop snarling at me. I did what I thought was best by agreeing to his plan on investigating your mole on my own," she replied. "God, Sanjeev was spitting mad when I confronted him. I don't know how, but he's determined to ruin me if I don't fall in line."

"You should've never gone to his office today," Ajay said. "Your safety is now at issue."

"Ajay, don't rile Hem up," she said.

"Oh, I'm way past riled up," Hem said. "Serious question, what did you hope to gain when he started threatening you?"

"I hoped to gain this," she said and slid her phone across the table. She pressed a button on the screen, and Sanjeev's voice came loud and clear through the speaker. If there was ever a quiet moment in New York City, it happened in that penthouse as the four of them listened to the recording.

Hem's anger shifted directions. Sanjeev, that rat bastard, was fucking with Hem's family just as much as he was fucking with Mina. There was no way he'd let that happen.

"I backed it up in a few places," Mina said when the recording ended. "You have proof that he's after Bharat, and I have proof that he's trying to ruin me. However, I think we need more evidence. Sanjeev is smart. He can argue against one tape."

Zail stood, pulling his phone from his pocket. "I have to talk to Sahar to shut down the team and make sure all the data is secure. Damn it. Does she know that we have a breach?"

"I couldn't hide it. I'm usually better about that, but we were both so stunned that we didn't have any pretenses about what was going on. She's going to start checking for security breaches when she reaches the office."

"Mina, have you told us everything?" Ajay said.

"Yes. Ajay. Zail. Hem. I can't even begin to tell you how sorry I am."

"I'm not," Ajay said. "Because of you, we're so much closer to nailing the bastard who's screwing with us. We also know that the board is dirty. And even if all of this doesn't lead us to the mole, we'll still help you hold Sanjeev accountable."

"Really? You—you will?"

"Of course. But you're the one who is going to have to report to the FBI. And I need your brain. If you help us, we'll wrap this up faster. I hope you're in for a long night."

She nodded. "I'm going to see if I have a contact at the Bureau, actually. I'll get the ball rolling first thing tomorrow morning with them. I'm also going to start wrapping up the due diligence report. I'll show it to you before I hand it in."

"Please." Ajay picked up his phone and made a call. "Rafael? Yes, can you come to my penthouse? Confidential issue that we have to deal with. Bring your laptop. I'm sending a car for you and Tiffany. We'll be working late."

When Mina left the table to get her computer, Hem followed her. "Come with me." He pulled her down a narrow hallway.

"Hem?" she said with a note of hesitation in her voice.

He knew he looked angry, that he practically radiated with it. He wanted to put a hole in Sanjeev's face and then make sure the bastard never breathed the same air as Mina again. But he had to control his fury because he had something more important to share with Mina right now.

He ushered her into Ajay's library filled with oak and leather furniture. When they were finally alone, he pressed her against the back of the door and dropped his forehead against hers. She let out a shuddering breath that mirrored his.

"Are you okay?" he finally asked.

"I should be asking you that. Don't you hate me?"

He let out a deep breath and braced his hands on either side of her head. "No, baby, I don't hate you," he said before dropping a kiss to her upturned mouth. "I'm mad as hell, at Sanjeev, at you for jeopardizing your safety, at this faceless traitor. No more secrets. We're going to figure this out together."

"I can't believe I've been so stupid this whole time," she said. Her breath hitched and a single tear slid down her cheek. "Deep down I knew Sanjeev wasn't going to give me the partnership so easily, but I still had hope. I was distracted. See, I told you! I told you that I needed to focus on work. We have to stop this. Stop us."

"Mina, you can't blame us just because it's convenient."

"I'm not! Can't you see? I knew this would happen."

"No, you didn't. You couldn't have, damn it. Anyone would've made the same mistake. Sanjeev is your family, and despite your history, you wanted to trust him."

"Hem, I still think—"

He covered her mouth with his, swallowing her protest. His heart swelled when Mina's fingers tangled in his hair, and tugged him closer. He closed his eyes, knowing that he was so desperate for her that he didn't think he'd ever get enough. And then, after almost losing control, he let go.

His hands smoothed over her shoulders, her hips,

trying to calm both of them from the rush of arousal. Hem still had things to say.

"We're a team," he started. "We're better together than we are apart."

"Hem—"

"No. Say it, Mina. Say it, and tell me you believe it."

He watched the struggle in her eyes, but she finally nodded and said, "We're a team. I believe you, Hem. It's just that if I'd only thought a few steps ahead. This is my mother's company and I feel it slipping away every moment of every day."

Hem brushed her tear away with the pad of this thumb. "Don't worry, hiriye. You'll still be able to keep your mother's legacy alive."

"How can I after all this?" She dropped her head back so it rested against the door. "I can't believe something so simple has become such a mess."

Hem thought about the report on her mother their investigators found, and he knew he couldn't bring it up yet. Even though he'd told her there were no more secrets between them, he'd have to wait.

"Hey," he said, cupping her face with one hand. "You'll find a way to remember your mother. Who knows? You may still get the law firm. Have you thought about bringing your dad in? Can he be trusted?"

"I—I don't know. My relationship with him has always been confusing. I think he helped Sanjeev and Kumar take the firm from my mother, but then Sanjeev admitted today that Dad is the reason why I have a job there in the first place. After we report Sanjeev, I feel like whatever chance of a relationship I have with him is going to suffer, too."

Hem kissed her again, this time deepening it until she softened against him. She wrapped her arms around his neck and he lost himself in her scent, in the silky feel of the ends of her braid, the slender curves of her body, the lush taste of her mouth.

When they pulled apart, they were both breathing a little heavy.

"Come home with me after this." He ran his hands over her hips and butt, squeezing her plump bottom until she let out a little gasp.

"I don't know if it's a good idea. It's been a long day, and with the way your brother is throwing out orders, it's going to be a long night."

Hem kissed her again, this time with a hint of desperation. "We're a team, remember? Come home with me. I want you in my bed. We have nothing to be afraid of."

Mina pressed her lips against his jaw. "Okay," she said.

The slight breathiness in her voice had him going rock hard in an instant, and he wanted to drag her home right then and there. But they had bigger issues to focus on, and figuring out the mole was becoming their number one priority.

When they reentered the living room, Zail was putting on his shoes.

"Where are you going?" Hem said.

"I called the jet. By the time I get to Teterboro, it should be ready. I have to get back to California and take care of things on the West Coast."

He came over and planted a kiss on Mina's cheek even as Hem tried to step between them. "Take care of yourself."

"Don't push it," Hem murmured.

"You're one to talk," Zail said with a grin. "I need info by Monday. In the meantime, I'm going to find Sahar." He waved at Ajay and slipped out the door moments later.

"Hem, the team that we had investigating the sales division has been put on notice," Ajay said from across the room. "I have our two lead cyber security investigators on their way here. We have six thousand employee documents to get through and that's just in the last four months. We're going to try to pull anything we can that is related to board members, too. If we can hack their laptops, we will."

Hem walked over to the dining room table and grabbed one of the remaining takeout containers that had noodles in it. He pried off the lid and put it in front of an empty chair for Mina. She surprised him when she walked over and slid into the seat he'd pulled out for her.

"What are you guys going to do when you find the leak?" she asked as she began picking at her noodles with a pair of chopsticks.

"We're going to hold the bastard accountable," Hem said. He looked up at his brother whose smile was just as grim, just as menacing. Hem wasn't part of the business anymore, but he was invested.

Not just for his father.

Not only for his brothers.

For Mina, too.

Then, he'd go back to the law firm he built, the firm he'd come to love, and start over with his woman.

Chapter Fifteen

IN A SHORT period of time, Mina's life went from a single-focused mission to a complicated mess. She usually didn't like messes. She preferred tidy, compartmentalized living. But when she remembered the empty mugs and dirty dishes scattered among computers, charging wires, and files she'd left at Ajay's home, she was utterly content.

It was three in the morning when Hem unlocked his penthouse front door. They'd stayed at Ajay's the longest. Tiffany and Rafael were the first to go. They'd helped pulling HR records and manually reviewing them for WTA ties. When Tiffany started to snore on her keyboard at midnight, Rafael escorted her home.

The cyber forensics crew left shortly after. They were still running tests through a remote access line and had to be up early in the morning to check the results.

Ajay was still on the phone, tablet in hand when they said their goodbyes. Mina was grateful that he'd let her help, but she'd also been ready to go. She wanted to decompress and spend some alone time with Hem. She still wasn't sure that continuing their relationship was a good idea while Bharat's future was at stake, but she had to learn how to trust the man she was falling in love with. If he was confident they could make it work, then she'd have to believe it, too.

As Hem turned on the lights from the com panel, he updated Zail on the phone about what they'd reviewed.

"The mole is good," Hem said. "The only thing Sri found so far is malware embedded in our systems. It's been there for about eight months, which is when we started losing sales opportunities. Now all we have to do is follow the audit logs."

"You still have to finish tracing large bank deposits for the Bharat employees and for the board of directors," Mina called out as she took off her leather jacket and collapsed on Hem's couch. "Follow the audit logs *and* follow the money."

Hem put his phone on speaker. "Did you hear that? Mina, repeat it to him."

She did and then added, "Also, I'm going to give you the same advice I gave your brothers. Stay out of the news while all of this is going on. I know the three of you normally stay out of the limelight, so keep doing whatever you need to so that you can maintain your privacy."

Zail's laugh was clear through the cell phone. "Media coverage is for the books. The billionaire lifestyle is glamorous when there is scandal, but for the most part, we just want to talk about stock prices."

"Well, if that doesn't just kill my Gideon Cross fantasies."

"Gideon who?" Hem said as he tugged the end of Mina's braid. "And why does it sound like I have to kill him?"

"Gideon Cross is a billionaire. Sylvia Day novels. Gideon owns the Crossfire building in the city, along with luxury high-rises, clubs, fitness centers, alcohol brands, resorts, you name it."

"He is definitely fictitious then," Zail said. "Besides. Who needs all that when we've got AI technology?"

"Sold!" Mina leaned over and pressed a kiss against Hem's cheek.

His expression darkened and he wrapped an arm around her waist to pull her close. Even though it was three in the morning, and Mina had been awake for twenty hours, desire wrapped around her like vine. Hem's hand gentled and stroked down her hip, tightening that vine until she was completely focused on him.

She reached up and ran a finger along his jaw.

"Zail, I'll talk to you tomorrow," he said.

She looked down at the phone that still rested in the palm of Hem's hand. "Thank you, Zail. For trusting me to help."

"Guddia, if my brother trusts you, how can I not?

Try to get *some* sleep. Knowing Ajay, he's going to need all of us tomorrow, too."

Hem said a few terse words to his brother in Punjabi before hanging up. In any other situation, she would have laughed, but she was too focused on Hem, and on the need that was growing between them despite the late hour.

Silence filled the penthouse. "I didn't know you enjoyed erotic romance," Hem said.

Mina laughed. "You do know Gideon Cross!"

"My legal assistant was obsessed with them a few months ago. Tell me, what part of those books did you like the most?"

Mina wrapped her arms around Hem. "The happily-ever-after part."

They stood, still wrapped around each other. Hem stroked her back from shoulder blade to waist before he said, "It's late and I know you've had quite a day."

When he'd kissed her at Ajay's house and told her that she should come home with him, Mina hadn't been sure if it was the right thing to do, but the longer the night progressed, the more she spent time with him, the more she knew that she was ready.

She needed Hem, needed to hold him and know that there was something good and right with the people that she chose to be with. She'd denied herself because she thought that was the only way she could focus on winning against her uncles. That staying away would keep her as a neutral party performing due diligence.

That no longer mattered. Discovering the truth about Sanjeev had helped set her free to pursue what she truly wanted to do, and she really wanted to lie in bed with Hemdeep Singh and welcome the sunrise.

She motioned for Hem to follow. He came to her, his eyes were those of a wild animal stalking prey. The feeling was breathtaking. They moved in silence down the hallway toward the master suite.

Mina's heart pounded with each step until they entered the dark bedroom.

"Turn master bedroom lights on low ambient," Hem said gruffly. The darkness faded to a candlelight glow. The curtains parted and the skyline, still flickering in beauty and vibrancy, stretched beyond the windows. The room smelled like Hem, heavy and rich with spice.

When she stood at the foot of the bed, Hem took her hands in his. "You've had a long night. We can just sleep."

"No," Mina said. "I trust you. I don't want to wait if I don't have to."

She reached for the hem of her shirt and pulled it over her head, exposing the La Perla he'd bought for her after their night at the club. His gaze grew fierce and her skin heated under it.

"You're perfect," he said, and reached out to brush a thumb against her turgid nipple. Mina leaned in to Hem's touch. "I want to feel you again."

"Well, that's all you're going to see until I get a view, too."

One black eyebrow arched at the statement. "Is that so?"

"Damn straight."

He reached behind his shoulders and yanked his T-shirt forward and over his head. Mina's eyes widened as he exposed more deep brown skin and taut muscles. He was beautiful, with crisp chest hair that tapered over his abdomen until a trail disappeared under the waistband of his jeans.

When was the last time Mina had felt this kind of desire that burned her from the inside out? She'd had affairs before, flings that were shorter than a train ride into Jersey. No one had ever captivated her, entranced her like Hemdeep Singh. He lifted a hand to remove her braid, and the glint of silver from his kara caught the light.

"You're perfect, too," she whispered. She stepped forward, running her fingers through his chest hair and over the muscles of his pecs and ridged abdomen. His arms came around her and he quickly unclasped her bra.

"Kiss me." The words weren't even out of her mouth before his mouth took hers. She felt consumed, and she was drowning with him, while all she could think was *finally.*

He pulled her bra straps down and over her shoulders until the lingerie was only held in place by the pressure of their bodies pressed together.

She wanted more of Hem, more skin, more everything. She reached for his belt and tugged it free. He sipped at her mouth, sucking at her lower lip as he made quick work of his clothes while she fumbled.

Then there was silky skin and his thick, hard cock. She pulled away, breathing heavy as she touched him for the first time. Her fingers wrapped around the base of his erection and stroked up the long length of him. A drop of precum beaded the head and Hem shuddered when she brushed her fingertip over it.

"My turn," he said, his voice raw with the same need Mina knew was in her own. He pulled back and yanked her bra away before kneeling to rid her of her jeans and panties. He leaned forward and pressed a kiss against her sex, dipping his tongue delicately into her wet heat.

"Hem," she sighed.

"Let's get comfortable," he said and stood. He ran his hands over her, touching her with barely restrained need. This was so much more intimate, so much more than she ever expected with Hem.

She gasped when he walked her backward and gently pushed her onto the bed. She bounced against the soft mattress and comforter before Hem stepped between her legs, grabbed her hips and moved her farther toward the headboard. She complied until he was kneeling between her spread thighs.

There was heat in his eyes, and something more, something she hoped would be there when he saw her like this. "Your tits," he said, running his hands over them and squeezing liberally. "Your tits are the most perfect shade of delicious brown that I have ever seen, and I want to taste them again."

"Yes," Mina gasped, lifting her chest for him.

She felt her pussy clench at the first hard suck. The feeling was so good that she raked her nails against Hem's back and pulled at his hair for all that he could give her.

Just when she was on the verge of climaxing from only the attention he'd paid to her breasts, he pulled away and ran two blunt fingers reached between her lips and dipped into her core. She shuddered at the intrusion of his fingers and the firm pressure he used to locate and rub her clit.

"You're wet," he said.

"Yes. Hem . . ."

"Tell me what you want."

"You know."

"Tell me, otherwise I'll stop."

"No! Hem . . . fuck me. Goddammit, fuck me."

"You want it hard and fast?" he asked, his voice as soft and smooth as the touch of his fingertips. Mina strained against him. "Or do you want it slow?"

She screamed when Hem pulled his fingers away. "No! Hem, more."

"Yes." Hem gripped Mina's hips and flipped her over onto her stomach. He yanked her onto her knees and held her steady even though her knees quivered.

She heard a foil wrapper tear, and she wondered for

a brief moment if he'd kept more than one in his night-stand drawer. Then he was sliding his cock against her, and all rational thought flew out the window.

"Now!" she panted.

"Now," Hem repeated and slid into her, stretching her muscles until she shook and sobbed from the pleasure-pain of it. He was so much thicker than she'd ever taken before. She clenched around him and heard his roar as he pulled out and pushed into her again, a little deeper this time. Mina pressed her face into the comforter, gasping with the sheer joy as she tilted her hips back so that she could take more of him.

Hem thrust again and this time seated himself all the way inside her. He filled her until she felt like he was part of her. The rightness, the overwhelming sensation of it, was frightening even as Mina rocked against him.

"Tell me you're mine," he said, panting just as hard as Mina.

She shook her head, thrashing against the pillow. He gripped her hips harder and pulled her against his cock, thrusting in earnest now until she screamed with pleasure and became delirious with it. She chanted his name, for him to fuck her harder, for him to take her. She gripped the sheets and writhed against him, until there was only Hem and the sounds of their bodies thrusting.

"You ever feel this before?" Hem asked, his words broken and barely audible. He changed his pace until he was able to say more clearly, "I'm yours. You're mine, Mina. We belong to each other."

"Hem," she gasped. "I'm going to come." Her hair hung over her face and she pushed back against him, harder and faster.

"Not until you tell me that you're mine."

"I'm—I'm yours!" The word came out as the orgasm rushed through her, tightening every muscle, exploding every pleasure point, until she was suspended in the moment. She thrust back against Hem, and he reached around her and brushed against her sensitive clit.

"Hem!" she screamed again as the pleasure continued to pulse through her, and then with two quick thrusts, he joined her. His chest pressed against her back, a cry erupting from his throat. They fell against the bed together, still connected.

She lay heavy and limp, her breathing harsh and her skin damp with a sweat. She hadn't known she could feel this way. It was obvious she wasn't having sex with the right people.

With Hem.

The shock settled over her as the impact of her orgasm began to fade.

Hem rolled off her back and, with a quick kiss against her shoulder, left the bed to go to the bathroom. She heard the toilet flush and then the sink running. He returned to the room with a damp cloth in his hand. Mina still hadn't moved, and she felt the faint tinge of embarrassment as he helped clean her. The warm cloth felt good against her tenderness, and she was humming with contentment by the time he finished.

Hem tossed the towel in a laundry basket and slipped back into the bed. Despite her height, he maneuvered her easily and pulled her against his chest until they were spooned together. They linked fingers and tangled limbs.

"It was worth the wait," she said softly.

Hem chuckled. "That was just the start."

"Mmm-hmm."

They lay in a comfortable silence until Hem let out a sigh and kissed the side of Mina's neck, inciting a trail of goose bumps. "I want to wake up with you like this and see the sunrise," he said.

"Well, you won't have to wait long," she said, looking over at the windows. The bright lights of the skyline began to dim as dawn approached.

They enjoyed the view in silence before Hem spoke.

"What's going through your mind?"

"Mmm."

"I want to know," he whispered against her ear. "What are your secrets?"

"I don't know if it's a secret, but I'm thinking that even though it's terrible how Bharat brought us together, I'm happy it happened."

"Why is that?"

"Because. Lying here with you, I know that every day can be like the Dosa Hutt."

She felt the muffled laughter in his chest before she heard it. "I have no idea what you mean, hiriye."

"Well, the Dosa Hutt represents believing in the impossible. With you, I know that I can believe in the impossible every day."

"Mina," he said gruffly. The raw emotion in his voice had her snuggling closer.

She was Mina Kohli, and she was determined to live her life the way she wanted. If that meant pursuing her mother's legacy or giving her heart to a Punjabi man, she'd do it.

She closed her eyes as Hem's breath began to even. She was Mina Kohli, and she was a warrior queen who'd finally found and fallen in love with her Sikh king.

Chapter Sixteen

MINA MADE LOVE with Hem two more times that night before she succumbed to exhaustion. She woke a few hours later to the feel of sunlight on her face and an empty bed beside her. When she reached out to touch where Hem had been, the sheets felt cool.

The clock read nine thirty, which mean that her lover was probably working. She had to work, too, but she wasn't sure if she should go to the Kohli and Associates office. It was Friday, and the likelihood that her uncles were remote was high, but Mina couldn't chance it. She would just have to check in with her legal assistant and paralegal and cancel any appointments.

She hugged Hem's pillow against her chest and took in a deep breath. Her life had shifted the night before, and she would never be the same again. Not just because of Hem, but because of the new shape of her future. She was going to report her uncles and hopefully secure Bharat from any more takeover attempts, but her goal for honoring her mother's legacy had to change.

Mina began working through her schedule as she stepped in the shower. She took a few moments to luxuriate in the bath products that Hem kept for her, then applied a little bit of makeup. After raiding his closet for the things he'd purchased for her, she put on a pair of jeans and a sleeveless white button-down shirt with a collar and a black bow at the neck. They were just a few of the items he'd stashed for her next to his white shirts and suit coats that hung in military order.

Half an hour later, she found him in the penthouse's loft office space, with a headset in one ear. He faced the wall of windows.

"I'll deal with it on Monday. No, this client is an important one. I'll be involved. There are a ton of capable people helping with my father's company that they shouldn't mind if I spend a few hours a day contributing to my own business needs."

He motioned for Mina to come forward when she reached the top of the stairs. The move was so utterly male, so dominant that she felt the need to say no at first simply on principle. But she wanted to be with him, to touch him, so she obliged. He pulled her close and she leaned against his side while he wrapped up the call.

"Morning, mera jivana," he said as he tossed his earpiece on the desk.

My life. She warmed at the sound of that and lifted

her mouth for a kiss. "Morning. You have more clothes for me in your closet."

"Really? I wonder who did that?"

She laughed. "Hem, we talked about this."

"Do you like them?" he asked.

Mina relented. "Yes. Thank you."

"You're welcome." His mouth softened as he smiled down at her, "You look beautiful. Are you hungry? We can grab some breakfast."

"Aren't you supposed to come up with a clever way to kick me out?"

He nipped at the tip of her nose. "Why would I do that when you're so fun to have around? You also have a great ass."

She slapped him on the chest. "Watch it, buddy."

"It goes both ways, you know. You get me, too." He took her hand and placed it over the semi that hardened further under her touch.

"And I intend to keep you for a while yet," she said with a quick stroke. "But I'm not sure about breakfast. I have to figure out what I'm doing today. Pretending everything is normal seems weird to me."

"Baby, I think that you don't have a choice for now. Not until the FBI acts on the report you file with them. We still have some time until the next board meeting and shareholders report."

Hem's phone buzzed on his desk, and Mina saw Ajay's name flash across the screen before Hem answered. "What's up?"

Ajay's voice came through loud and clear. "Brahm is headed toward the estate."

"What? What the hell is he doing in the US?"

"Apparently he has urgent news. Zail can't make it but you need to head back to Alpine. I'm already on my way."

Hem looked down at Mina. "I'll leave in five. I just have to drop Mina off first."

Before Mina could motion to him that she'd take a cab, Ajay was already protesting. "Bring her with you. She's sharp, and she'll help us fill in the gaps that we can't see."

"Bring Mina to Alpine?" The stunned expression on his face, the rejection in his eyes was noticeable. "I don't think that's necessary."

Even though their relationship was new, his reaction hurt. There was no question that it was too soon to meet his parents, but Hem made it seem as if it was never a possibility. She tried to suppress the ache in her chest.

"Mina, wait. Ajay, how much work will we be getting done if we're at the estate?"

"If I have it my way, we'll finish this. Dad can hopefully help."

"Okay, if that's the case, I'll bring her. We'll be there soon." He pocketed his cell this time and stepped toward her. "Don't look like that. Please."

"No, it's completely fine. We definitely don't need to add family to the mix right now."

He shook his head. "You've never had parents like

mine. They've . . . they can ruin relationships, and I want you all to myself before they start meddling."

In the short time she'd come to know Hem, she'd been able to read his moods and reactions. He was thinking that she'd react just like Lisa had when she met the Singhs. It hurt that he wouldn't trust her, wouldn't believe in her to stay with him.

"I should go home. You can always fill me in later."

"If Ajay thinks you should be there, it's going to be business through and through. I'll protect you. Unless you want to leave?"

When she didn't say anything, he cupped her face and tilted her head up to meet his kiss. "I'm sorry. He just took me by surprise. Come with me. I want more time with you. You can use your laptop or cell to answer any emergencies you need to address with your case files."

She hesitated, but he kissed her again, and how could she say no to that? "Okay, if that's what you want."

"Yes," he said. "This is what I want."

"Then let's go."

They packed work bags with their computers and were on their way out the door within five minutes. Mina decided to focus on her inbox and get some work done to pass the time on the drive. She'd received over eighty new emails since her lunch the day before, but thankfully, her legal assistant flagged her messages in order of importance.

In forty-five minutes, Mina managed to make her

way through most of her mail. She shut down her laptop when Hem maneuvered the car through the ornate gates of the Singh estate.

"Holy shit," she said as she took in the gardens and the home in the distance.

"Yeah."

"Hem . . . this is Bharat Mahal?"

"Yup. It was Dad's dream to have a big enough place for all of his brothers and their children to visit once a year for a reunion. What really ended up happening was that he takes a trip back to Punjab. He gets homesick for the smell of mustard fields and sugarcane."

Hem veered off toward the left and soon they were passing the most enchanting colonial homes. Mina gasped when Hem pulled into the third driveway. "Is this yours?"

"It is. I figured we'd leave the car here and walk to the main house. It's not that much farther on foot."

"Can we go to your place first?"

Hem looked puzzled, but he motioned to his front door. "If you want."

"Yes, I definitely want, Hem." She walked up the short path to the porch and entered through the front door. She gasped when she opened it. The inside was like something out of a fairy tale. Her parents' house used to have the same charm, but as she'd grown older, the house grew dull and lacked the life it once had.

"Do . . . do you like it?" Hem asked as he stood in the entrance.

"Like it? I *love* it." She traveled from room to room, brushing her fingertips over surfaces and textures. She ended up in the kitchen. "Your penthouse is amazing, but this is so damn beautiful. Why don't you spend more time here?"

"I used to," he said. "I even brought an ex here, but she preferred the penthouse."

"I'm not Lisa. The city is amazing, but this is where I'd be on weekends."

His shoulders relaxed, as if he'd been waiting for her reaction this whole time. She was about to say something, but Hem's cell buzzed and he turned to check the readout. "Ajay is getting antsy. Let's go."

He led her outside and down the path to the main house. Mina's astonishment grew as they walked through the double doors, but all her joy faded when they heard shouting from the foyer.

"Shit," Hem said.

Mina matched his long strides until they were in the biggest kitchen and living space she'd ever seen.

"What is going on?" Hem said. His words fell on deaf ears.

An older woman, a man in a suit with movie star hair, and Ajay shouted at each other in Punjabi and English. The unmistakable Mr. Deepak Singh looked ashen and sat in silence. He wore a white kurta pajama and a beige shawl that wrapped around his shoulders.

Hem tried again to get everyone's attention but they were too busy yelling at each other to hear. Mina stuck two fingers in her mouth and let out a piercing whistle. The room fell into complete silence from one heartbeat to the next.

"I can't believe that worked," she said.

"Thanks. Now. Can anyone tell me what the hell is going on?" Hem repeated. When they all began talking at once, he made a T shape with his arms. "One at a time, damn it. Ajay? What's happening?"

"Brahm came here to tell us about our dearest uncle Gopal," he said.

"What about him?"

Brahm shoved his fingers through his perfect hair. "The bastard sold his shares of Bharat to WTA for top dollar. WTA now has a sizeable amount of shares in our company. They're a major shareholder."

"What the hell? How did Gopal get Bharat shares?"

Everyone turned to look at Deepak. The old man stared into space, looking defeated and worn. The image was completely different from the framed magazine covers in the foyer of Bharat's offices.

"Pa-ji," Hem said softly. "Please tell me you didn't."

"He needed to focus on the family and not on his drug addiction," Deepak said in Punjabi. "It was supposed to help him gain a vested interest in working for the company."

"Well, that sure as hell didn't work did it, Chacha?" Brahm snapped. "I'm here to tell you that you can't save him. Not anymore."

Ajay and Hem started in unison, but it was the older

woman who quieted the room this time. She stared at Mina as she yelled, "Enough! I didn't realize that we had . . . company."

She walked toward Mina and reached out to touch her hands. "I'm Hem's mother," she said in English. "I'm sorry about this scene you've just witnessed. My son has better sense usually and warns the family so we're all on our best behavior."

Mina responded in Punjabi. "I'm working as an attorney at Bharat right now, Auntie-ji. I'm well aware of all three of your sons' temperaments. No need for such formality with me."

The woman's eyes filled with tears and Mina backed away, not sure what to do.

Luckily, the British man intervened. "Mina, right?" He came over and extended his hand. "Brahm. I run the UK office."

"Nice to meet you."

"Can we focus for a second?" Ajay said. "We need to know exactly how many shares and if WTA is making a move to buy the twenty-five percent we released to the public."

"Dad," Hem said. "Tell us everything. Now."

"Hem, leave him be," his mother said.

"No, this is serious. He could be tanking our chances of stopping WTA. At this point we may have to sell off parts of the business."

"You're not in charge anymore," Deepak said, his voice laced with a venom that hushed the room. "You left, remember? You left me and the business because of a woman. And now you've come back, because of a woman? I will not hear anything from you."

"Deepak!" Hem's mother snapped. "Watch yourself."

"And he may not be in charge anymore, but I am," Ajay said. "And I want those answers."

The brief respite was over, and the shouting continued, but this time, Deepak was raising his voice, too. His anger seemed to focus on Hem.

"I told you going public was a bad idea, Dad!"

"You only said that because Lisa gave you that advice."

"Actually she agreed with you. I formulated my own opinions, and it looks like I was right after all."

"She drove you away, Hem!"

"No, damn you, you drove me away. You're using her as an excuse! I did the same, but at least I can admit it."

"Blame us, blame *me* for your own wrongdoing. What will you do if this girl drives an even bigger wedge between us? When she leaves, will you blame us, too, for something we haven't done?"

"This is not about Lisa and Hem," Ajay said. "Dad, you got us into a mess, and we're here to get out of it. Hem is here to help."

"Yes, I'm solely responsible for WTA," he shouted. "Blame me for losing the company. Do you think I intended for this to happen? I made this company the way it is!"

"And you're doing a good job at screwing it over, too," Hem snapped.

Deepak said something, but the words were lost in a coughing fit. The voices around the room quieted when Deepak started gasping. He clutched his arm and tipped out of his chair. Everyone moved at once. Time slowed, and Hem barely made it to his father's side before he crumbled to the floor.

"Call 911," he shouted, but Ajay already had his phone out.

Brahm held back Hem's mother who began to sob in her shawl. "Deepak!" she cried.

The housekeeper came running in and Mina intercepted him. "Please make sure the front gate is open, and there is a car ready," she said.

"We need them here now," Ajay roared. "We can call the helicopter."

"Too slow," Hem said. "Ambulance is our best option."

Her heart pounded as she watched the scene helplessly, the fear on Hem's face, the glassy loss of focus on Ajay's, and the shock on Brahm's handsome features. She ended up holding Hem's mother at one point as she sobbed into Mina's shoulder.

Long, agonizing minutes passed until the ambulance finally came and Deepak was loaded onto a stretcher. Mina followed everyone outside and to the car. She was about to get into the back of one of the vehicles when Hem stopped her.

"Take the Tesla back to my place. Or I'll have our housekeeper order a car for you."

"Hem, I want to go to the hospital with you."

"No," he said. His lips thinned, and his eyes were wild with panic. "No, I don't want you here with my family. I should've never brought you."

"Hem, you don't mean that. I can help."

"You were right, damn it. You need to focus on Bharat and not on me. You can't afford to make another mistake. Go home and get to fucking work, Mina."

Ajay called Hem's name and he slipped into the passenger seat of the sedan without a backward glance. The car roared down the drive and Mina was left standing at the base of the steps, reeling from Hem's rejection.

Chapter Seventeen

HEM KNEW HE'D screwed up the moment the panic and fear cleared from his brain.

He sat in the plush leather chair of the private waiting room, the one reserved for people who were shelling out major cash for the welfare of family members, and closed his eyes. He shouldn't have told Mina to go. She'd only been trying to help.

He heard the chair next to him squeak and looked over to see Ajay collapse next to him. "What a day."

"Any info from the nurses?"

"No, just that Dad's stable. Relapsing from congestive heart failure means that his recovery time is now going to be longer."

"Shit."

"I know. But it's not as bad as we thought. He'll be okay. The doctors are confident."

"He's going to be pissed when he's healthy again."

Ajay nodded. "As cruel as it sounds, with Dad busy getting better, we'll be able to fight a little dirty and find out how WTA is screwing us."

"Don't talk like that with Mom around, man."

"Brahm is with her in the cafeteria. They're trying to get some chai."

Hem closed his eyes again. "This is a disaster."

"No, you're a disaster," Ajay said.

He turned to his brother again. "What the hell does that mean?"

"You shouldn't have sent Mina away, man. She was handling things like a pro."

Even though his thoughts were along the same lines, he felt the need to defend his decision. It wasn't his brother's job to tell him how he'd messed up a relationship that was more important to him than anything else he'd experienced before. "You saw how Dad reacted to her presence. She was only going to make things worse by coming to the hospital with us."

"Dad was reacting that way because of you, not Mina. He trusts your leadership more than he's ever trusted mine. He was ignoring me and Brahm before you showed up. Then when you started asking the same questions, he got defensive."

Hem let out a breath. He knew that Ajay was still struggling to prove himself, and his father wasn't cutting him any breaks. After the last couple months, Hem truly believed that Ajay belonged at Bharat more than he ever had before. "He may not show it, but he respects you. I've been with him at the helm for a lot longer, and that's the only reason why he'll hear me out first. It'll take time, but once he wakes up from his stupidity, he'll see that you are so much better at this job than all of us."

"I hope so." Ajay nudged him in the arm. "Tell me something. Is it true that Lisa thought we should go public?"

"Yes," he said. "She said I was making a huge mistake by leaving the company when it had so much promise."

"She was right. The numbers don't lie, Hem. We're just as deadly as the worst of the sharks in these waters."

"I see that. And if anyone can turn this around, it's you. It's also clear I don't belong at Bharat. I have other dreams and the longer I'm helping Bharat, the more I know that I made the right decision to leave."

"Does Mina agree?"

"Mina . . . yeah. Yeah, she believes in the impossible for me. Or at least she used to until I basically told her to get lost and that she's a screw up. Man, I really fucked it up today."

They slipped into a silence, the sounds and smells of the hospital around them. No matter how plush they made the private waiting room, the facility was still a hospital.

"Are you going after her?" Ajay finally asked.

"I'm going to try."

"She's good for you, brother. Both of you work like a unit. I can see that she makes you happy. Do us all a favor and don't make her pay for the mistakes you made with Lisa."

Hem nodded, his brother's words a truth that weighed on his shoulders. "It's so much more complicated than that."

Ajay switched to Punjabi when one of the cleaning crew came in to change out the garbage. "I know we don't talk about things like 'feelings' but I have some advice for you. I know you hold Mom and Dad accountable, but with the way you and Lisa were going, they just happened to be an easy scapegoat for how your relationship ended. Our parents will never change. They're stubborn and brilliant. Mina is stubborn and brilliant, too. She can handle them in ways that your ex never could."

Hem looked down at the bracelet he always wore and ran his finger over the metal. A kara was a symbol of strength, a reminder to always keep his guru's teachings in mind and to do what was right.

"What makes you think Mina is more accepting than my ex?"

"Are you serious? Like Lisa, Mina didn't have the same upbringing we did, but she understands you, and that's what makes her different."

Hem had spent so long repressing memories of his ex-girlfriend that now, when he recalled some of the complaints she'd had, he had to agree that Mina would never say the same things.

Things are moving too fast. Do normal people even have multi-day flashy weddings?

Who lives with their parents at our age?

I can't do this anymore, Hem. I can't be your girlfriend and share you with your parents, your brothers and your religion anymore.

You're making a big mistake. How could you even think about leaving Bharat?

Hem realized that his intelligent, witty, Punjabi queen didn't judge him like that.

She was the one. Mina Kaur Kohli was the girl for him because she accepted him for who he was. She saw possibilities with him, and she made him laugh. She should've been the first woman he'd introduced to his parents. He couldn't change the past, but he had every intention of keeping her in his future.

"Do you think she'll stick around?"

Ajay laughed. "Brother, if she's lasted this long, I think she's in it for life. You're lucky. In the little bit of time we've worked together, it's clear that she's an amazing woman."

"Damn straight."

The double doors opened and Brahm escorted Hem's mother into the room. They each held a cup of chai in hand.

"I'm going to go check with the nurses," Hem's mother said.

"Mom, I just checked," Ajay replied. "He's stable."

She muttered something in Punjabi about sons who don't know how to keep their mouths shut and crossed to the nurses' station at the other end of the room.

Brahm hitched up his pinstriped pants and sat in the chair on the other side of Hem. He put his cup in one of the holders and lifted the chair's mechanical footrest. His rainbow socks peeked out between Ferragamo shoes and slim-fit dress pants.

"Chachi is a demon. I don't know how you guys live with her."

"What did she do now?" Ajay asked.

"She asked if I'd found any sensible Indian boys to marry in the UK."

Hem snorted. "I think she wants you to get married more than she wants us to."

"Because she knows that when I get married, it's going to be classic and elegant. I'd have something like a traditional Punjabi ceremony with a vineyard backdrop. You three blokes are probably going to have keg stands and beat your chests during the milni."

Ajay laughed. "Brahm, the whole purpose of the wedding milni is to meet the brothers, cousins, and uncles of the other family and prove that we're stronger and better and staking a claim on one of their women. Beating chests is part of the ritual."

"See what I'm saying? Heathens, the lot of you."

"Your upper-crust British bullshit is too much right now," Hem said.

Brahm slapped him on the shoulder. "Chutiya, you're only saying that because you look like a sad, kicked puppy. Why don't you go to her? In all honesty, I expected you to have left already."

Hem faked a nut shot that had Brahm jackknifing in his seat. Ajay and Hem burst into laughter as their cousin straightened his suit jacket.

"Fuck you," he said in his crisp accent.

"You deserved it."

His cousin was right about needing time to beg for forgiveness. However, there was one last thing he had to address before he left. "Brahm, what happened to Gopal?"

Brahm's face grew solemn. "He's in rehab near Bath. His therapist said that he's over the withdrawal and he's suffering from depressive mood disorder. He's getting the help he needs, though."

"How did you find out about the shares?" Ajay asked.

"I went to see him yesterday. He was sobbing. He said that a few days before I extracted him from Punjab, he'd been approached by a WTA representative. They offered twice the amount they were worth. Gopal wanted the money, so he sold the shares."

"Son of a bitch," Hem said.

"There's more," Brahm said. "This is what I really didn't want to send over email or even a phone call. I took care of Gopal's dealer when the extraction happened. He was starting to threaten the family. Our cousins, the ones that still talk to me anyway, were ready to take out their shotguns."

Ajay stood. "Thanks, Brahm. That's one less thing we now have to worry about."

"Not quite. Some intel I received says that the dealer

was paid to target the family. They had to find the weakest link and report back to another person."

"Do you think it's WTA?" Hem said. "Were they the ones who tried to get to Deepak through his brothers?"

"Maybe. I'll keep digging but I don't know anything for sure yet."

If Brahm's intel was right, the corporate giant had made a critical mistake. They'd purposely targeted family, and now that it was personal, Hem and his brothers were going to go above and beyond to fight back.

"Thanks for all your help," Ajay said. He pulled out his phone and began typing. "We figure out the percentage that WTA now owns, and then we come up with a plan. We can't wait any longer to clean house."

"What does that mean?" Hem asked.

"It means we move up the board meeting to next week."

"I'm just as invested in the future of Bharat and the family as you two are, so I'll stay for a few days and see if I can help with developing a strategy to fight," Bhram said.

"Use Zail's office in New York for the week."

Brahm grinned. "It'll be good to see your assistant again, Ajay."

"If Rafael quits or brings sexual harassment charges against you, I'll personally snap off your dick."

"Harsh, and completely not necessary. Raphael was interested once. I just have to remind him of what he liked back then."

Hem stood as well, WTA still on his mind. "On a more serious note, I'll talk to some of my contacts and see if we have any recourse. I'll ask Mina if she has suggestions on how to deal with this, too."

"Speaking of Mina," Ajay said. "Weren't you on your way to beg for her forgiveness?"

"Yeah, yeah. Just you wait until you find a woman worthy of groveling to. You'll do it as gladly as I am, if it makes her happy."

"When hell freezes," Ajay said dryly. "Say hi to Mina for me."

"I won't. Let me know if Dad's situation changes."

"Where are you going?" His mother's voice had him turning around. She was still a little pale and cupped her chai in both hands. Hem went to her and rubbed his hands down her arms.

"I'm going to check on Mina."

Her face brightened. "Mina. What's her last name?"

"Kohli."

"Sikhini?"

"Yes, Mom," he said, rolling his eyes.

"I like her."

Despite the dire circumstances his family was embroiled in at the moment, he couldn't help but laugh at his mother's obvious excitement. "You'd like a paper bag as long as it was a Punjabi Sikh paper bag."

She called him an idiot in both Hindi and Punjabi. Only a Punjabi mother could make an insult sound like an endearment. "You should've warned me that you were bringing her to the house. I'm so ashamed of what we said in front of her. And your father! I'll straighten him out the minute he's better. I don't know what's wrong with that man. Mina shouldn't have seen the fight. I don't want what happened with Lisa to—"

"Mom," Hem said. "Mina isn't my ex. She's made of stronger stuff. I truly believe that she can handle whichever way you want to welcome her." He pulled his mother in for a hug, and some of the resentment he'd carried around for over a year dissipated. He leaned down and kissed the top of his mother's head. "You be who you are. Family means accepting people's true self, even if my Muma and Pa-ji are drama queens."

Hem felt his mother sniffle against his chest, and he held her closer. This proud, amazing woman who'd raised a family and stood by Deepak Singh, one of the most brilliant minds in technology, deserved to feel respected and loved for who she was. Mina would understand.

"I'll call you tomorrow," he said. "I'll also come out again if anything changes with Dad."

"Okay. Drive carefully."

Hem was across the room and opening the double doors when his mother called his name again. "Take her some food."

"What?"

"Take her some food. She won't turn you away if you try to feed her. It's impolite."

He knew he'd be facing an uphill battle because of

the way he'd dismissed Mina from the estate. Because Mina wasn't going to let him get off the hook easily, he was willing to try new things. Bringing food wasn't all that terrible a suggestion.

"Thanks, Mom," he said and slipped through the double doors. It was time to grovel.

Chapter Eighteen

MINA HAD NEVER cried over a man. She had more important things to do with her time than waste it on tears. But when she walked back to Hem's bungalow and saw the pretty painted shutters and remembered the way that Hem smiled at her when they stood in his foyer together, she let out a strangled sob. Just when she'd fallen in love with the idiot, he broke her heart.

When she stopped feeling sorry for herself and for the fact that she was most definitely in love with an idiot, her anger began to displace the hurt. There she was, stranded in Alpine, when what she really needed to do was figure out how to make sure she'd keep her law license and her job.

With that in mind, Mina decided that calling a car wasn't nearly as satisfying as driving the Tesla. She had the keys, and she figured that if she got a ticket, Hem could pay for it. His car, his problem.

She spent the first leg of the drive swearing, and the second falling into a surreal calm. The turnpike gave her time to think and to focus on what she wanted to tell Hem when he came back. Despite the hurt that still festered in her heart, she was feeling marginally better by the time she reached the tunnel.

When her phone pinged, she answered right away. "Hello?"

"Mina? Hi, it's Virat."

Another man she didn't want to deal with, she thought. "Virat? Hi, what can I help you with?"

"I wanted to make sure that you were still available for dinner tonight."

The dinner. She'd completely forgotten that she agreed to see him after the chaos of the day before. She was about to say no, because she desperately wanted to go back to her condo and wallow, but it wasn't fair to Virat to keep prolonging the inevitable. She had to cut ties with him before her uncles made the decision for her.

"Sure, I can still meet, but there was a change in plans. I'm not at my office today. A . . . friend had a family emergency and I had to go to New Jersey to help. I'll be working remote for the rest of the day."

"That's fine," Virat said. "Is there another location more convenient?"

She took a minute to think. She was flying down the

West Side Highway, which meant that she'd be home within ten minutes. "There's a wine bar across from my apartment building. If you can meet at the same time we agreed upon, we'll be able to get a table. It'll be quiet."

"That works for me." Six thirty would give Mina just enough wiggle room to decompress in her apartment.

"Great," she said.

"Good. Looking forward to it." He said a goodbye and hung up.

Mina wondered how transparent she had to be with Virat. She really wanted to come out and say, *Dude. I'm not going to marry you, so you should probably look elsewhere.* The problem was, she didn't know whether he'd be that open to her bluntness.

Mina's phone pinged again and this time she checked the readout before answering.

"Raj? Perfect timing. I really need to bitch to someone about how much I hate men."

"Me, too," her friend said in a tired tone. "But unfortunately, we need to talk about business."

"What kind of business?"

The sound of a keyboard clicking echoed through the phone. "The kind that affects your new man. I received an interesting call from a colleague who said that parts of Bharat's organization might be for sale soon. There is a new majority shareholder who is looking to oust the CEO and take the company in a different direction."

It was obvious that WTA was already looking to

start a hostile takeover. Mina sighed. "Thanks for that, Raj. I appreciate your help."

"There's more. One of WTA's C-suite executives is related to a Bharat employee."

Mina almost crashed into the car in front of her. In all the documents and paperwork that she and the Bharat team had reviewed, not once had they seen any connection between a Bharat employee and WTA.

"*Who?*"

"Her name is Sahar Ali Khan. She's head of Research and Development at Bharat."

"Oh my god," Mina said. She pinched the bridge of her nose. "This is a disaster." She updated her friend on everything that had happened since the previous day. Raj let out a low whistle when she mentioned that Sahar knew about the leak.

"You are in some deep waters, babe," Raj said. "It makes sense that Sahar would be the leak because of her connections and her access to information. I'm going to email you a few documents. Just make sure the information checks out, otherwise you're going to condemn an innocent person."

"The only person I want to condemn is my uncle Sanjeev."

"My security team has contacts with law enforcement and the Bureau if you want to use them."

Mina laughed, and it was the first time all day that she truly appreciated some humor. "Why do you have all these connections, Raj? I spent hours with Ajay and

Hem's security people and we couldn't find anything. But you call me with news in less than twenty-four hours."

"If Ajay's people can't come up with basic information like mine have, then Ajay needs to fire them," Raj said. Her voice was hard and flat. There was no doubt that Raj was a leader through and through. "You don't make money if you play nice. Those Singh brothers are smart, and I hope they figure this all out soon. Keep me posted and let me know if you need my help."

"Will do," Mina said.

After valet parking Hem's car in the garage next to her apartment building, she decided to use the time she had before meeting Virat to review the information Raj had emailed. As she read, it became clear that Sahar had motive and opportunity to leak her research. There were still so many unanswered questions, though. Why wouldn't she simply take her skills to WTA instead of working at Bharat and then putting her whole career on the line? Was there something else that WTA wanted? Was Sahar the decoy?

Mina was still working through the details when she walked across the street and into Vino's. The trendy Hell's Kitchen wine bar was packed with employees enjoying happy hour specials. The bar was a deep honey gold, and Edison light bulbs with iron cage chandeliers hung from the ceiling. It was a beautiful meeting place and conveniently located. She just wished she was drinking under better circumstances.

After scanning the crowd, she saw Virat in a blue suit at one of the high tables along the back-left side of the bar. His face lit up when he saw her.

"It's great to see you again," Virat said when Mina approached the table. He stood and leaned forward to kiss her cheek.

"Thank you," Mina replied. She slid into the empty chair and hooked her ankles on the bottom rung. "Sorry about the quick change of plans."

"I don't mind. Would you like a drink?"

"Please," she said.

The waitress appeared a moment later with her tablet. "What can I get you?"

"Do you have any suggestions for a white wine?" Virat asked.

"Saffron Fields Riesling is our most popular right now."

"I'll take that. Mina?"

She practically tossed the menu on the table. "Any Riesling other than Saffron Fields."

She knew that both Virat and the waitress were staring at her but she didn't care.

"I guess we should've gone for the champagne," Virat said when they were alone again.

"Why is that?"

He shot her a confused look. "Because we're celebrating our engagement."

His words were as effective as a slap across the face. "*What?* Virat, I haven't said yes."

"You haven't?" Virat's jaw dropped. "But—but Sanjeev informed my father yesterday that you accepted the arrangement and that we're supposed to look at wedding dates in the next six months! Mina, my parents are working with the firm's communication team to make a formal announcement."

Mina's jaw dropped. "And you didn't think for a moment how strange it was that I hadn't called you right away? That we hadn't talked first?"

Virat's face turned ruddy, and after he scanned their surroundings, he leaned across the table and lowered his voice. "Mina, this whole time while you've been working on your due diligence project, Sanjeev and my father have taken the majority of the planning and have been simultaneously drafting merger documents. He's giving us most of what we want, so we're just about ready to sign."

Mina covered her face with a groan. Her uncle was using Virat as a decoy, a distraction for her, while he set her up as scapegoat for the Bharat case. She knew her weaknesses, her tendency to have tunnel vision when she got involved in a project. Apparently, Sanjeev knew her weaknesses, too. Virat had been a red herring all along. If she hadn't told the Singhs about her mission and they hadn't shared the workload, she would've been too focused on one case or another to notice her uncle's plan.

When she looked back up at Virat, his face had gone stone serious as the waitress approached the table, left two wineglasses, and disappeared. She must have sensed the stress between them.

"Virat—"

"No," he said. His voice was sharp and more authoritative than she'd ever heard before. He picked up his glass and downed half the contents. "No, Mina," he started again. "Don't make excuses and please don't try to placate me. You never intended to agree to the marriage in the first place."

Mina shook her head. She had two options: she could take the risk and tell Virat the truth about her situation, or she could create a lie about the validity of the merger and whether complicating business with pleasure was the right path.

There were so many lies, so much bullshit in her life at that moment, that she had to bet on the truth.

"I thought about it from a practicality standpoint," she finally said. "My sole purpose was to obtain a partnership position at my mother's firm, and the merger was the ticket to achieving my goal."

He let out a jagged breath, frustration and anger blazing in his eyes. "In the times we spoke, just you and me, why didn't you say something? I thought you were as interested in the marriage as I was, damn it."

"You didn't exactly seem very forthcoming yourself. You were going along with whatever your parents wanted for you."

"I deserve that." Virat pointed to his glass and ticked two fingers in the waitress's direction. "I deserve that," he repeated. "So now we're here, after months of nego-tiation, back to square one."

"Are we? I just showed you my cards. Now it's time for you to show me yours. You can't seriously be mad that we aren't getting married. Did the merger mean that much to you?"

They sat for a few moments in silence. Virat twirled his empty wineglass in hand, and when he received an-other drink, he sipped it this time. "I want my father to retire," he finally said. "The bastard can't let go, and I deserve to run that firm. He doesn't trust me to do it on my own."

It was obvious that he was telling the truth. Some of the tension released in her shoulders as she sank back in her seat. If they had a similar goal, one that didn't in-volve marriage itself, maybe he'd have input that could help her with her situation.

"You think the merger is going to push your father out of the picture."

"I know it will. He said that with me married and with another lawyer by my side, I'll be able to handle the immigration arm, and one day the whole legal empire. I don't care about the entire business, but I deserve to lead the client base I built."

"Trust me, you don't want anything to do with my mother's firm . . . no, with Sanjeev's firm," she said. Her heart broke a little when she admitted the truth out loud. With all the damage Sanjeev had done, it was hard to see Kohli and Associates as a representation of good or a representation of her mother's work.

"The merger will definitely satisfy my father. But if you don't want to get married, then I can't force you. Shit. *Shit*."

Mina reached out and grabbed his hand. She needed to tell him about the firm, about what he wanted and why it was so wrong. Trusting him could be dangerous, but there was something about Virat's reaction that made her feel like they were kindred spirits.

"I'm about to tell you something in confidence. It could cost me my license, and if that happens, I'll have a few very angry Punjabi men looking for you. Which, by the way, isn't as scary as I can be."

His eyes widened. "Fine. Tell me."

"Let's say hypothetically there was a case I was working on for a company. And hypothetically, a managing partner at my firm you may or may not know, has some inside knowledge about this case." She gave Virat the high-level overview of what her uncle was involved in. Trusting him with any ammunition that her uncle could use against her was a risk, but it paid off when she saw the disgust in his face.

"What are you going to do?" he asked after she finished. "About this hypothetical case I mean." He'd run his hands several times through his hair, contributing to a mussed look that was the antithesis of what he'd always presented himself.

"I'm still working on that. All I know is that I have to report Sanj—I mean this managing partner. I have a friend who offered to help, but even then, it could be weeks or months."

"Wait a minute." Virat sat up a little straighter, his eyebrows furrowing at a thought. "I know someone who can help you."

"Help me with what?"

"With your report. She's a . . . friend at the economic espionage and trade secrets division of the FBI. She transferred over there after she left USCIS a couple months ago. I'm happy to share her contact information with you. Honestly, I'm glad you told me what's going on. You saved my firm from what sounds like a terrible business deal. Hypothetically of course. Let me help by giving you a contact."

Virat smiled, and the genuine expression brightened his face. For the first time since Mina met him, she realized that his boyish looks were charming. He might be shorter than her, but so was most of the world's population. And most important, he wasn't running off to tell Sanjeev what she'd said.

Mina shook her head. "It's not an equal trade-off. I'll still be indebted to you for giving me a shortcut to kicking Sanjeev out of the picture."

"Maybe, after this is all done, you can help me come up with a solution for how I can get rid of my father." When the waitress came over one last time, he asked for the check and discreetly slipped her his credit card.

"Have you asked him bluntly to get out?" Mina asked when the waitress left.

Virat laughed. "Of course not. He's my father."

"And you're the nice son who does what he's told, whose mother serves him food at the table, and who probably lives in an apartment over the garage. Maybe acting outside the norm might be your only chance at proving how much of a leader you are."

He let out a deep breath, even though his face was flushed with embarrassment. "Well, this situation is definitely outside the norm. Maybe it's a starting point for a longer conversation."

"Prove your confidence. Tell him it's your turn."

When the waitress returned, he signed the check and then escorted her out of the wine bar and onto the sidewalk. The night air was chilly, but Mina didn't seem to mind. She felt lighter and more at peace. One problem resolved, one more in the form of Bharat to go.

"I'm going to tell my father tomorrow about nixing the merger," Virat said. "Let me get the ball rolling. In the meantime, I can connect you with Josette Hu. Josette will be able to expedite Sanjeev's case."

"Do you want to text her or call her so that she knows to expect me?"

"I can do that," Virat said. He looked across the street at Mina's building and back at her. "But I actually have a better plan—"

"I'm listening."

"Can I make a suggestion as a friend to another

friend? If you have some whiskey, we can call Josette together. I'm intrigued about how she plans on dealing with your uncle's fuckery."

"Hypothetically," they said in unison.

Virat let out a laugh. "Immigration law is never this exciting. And truthfully? I could really use something stronger than wine."

Mina laughed. "I'll order pizza, too. But you have to get Josette on the phone to stay."

"Yeah, she'll pick up my calls. She has the same suggestions you do. That I should move out and stand my ground against Dad."

"If you're open to them, I have a few more. Like how you're never supposed to tell a woman that you don't like it if she wears heels, especially if she's taller than you."

Virat groaned. "That's a thing?"

"Oh you have so much to learn, friend." They walked side by side across the street.

Chapter Nineteen

HEM WAS EXHAUSTED by the time he got to the city. He went straight to Mina's apartment building, and after a brief stare-down with the security guard, took the elevator to her floor. He hadn't texted her, because he wanted to grovel in person. When he approached her front door, ready for a confrontation, he heard laughter.

Male laughter.

Mina's voice followed. Even though her words were muffled, Hem could tell that she was happy.

He'd expected her to be angry or upset, but happy? Not on his radar. It was obvious that her joy was coming from another man, and that was . . . painful to realize. His breath exploded from his body. He'd hurt her, and he'd regretted it the moment his stupidity cleared. Would Mina turn her back on him so quickly? He'd treated Mina poorly because he'd expected her to react like his ex. Was it too late?

No. No way. He couldn't go there. There had to be an explanation, damn it.

His hands fisted when that male laughter echoed again, and he pounded on the door. The noise inside silenced, and he heard approaching footsteps. He knew the moment Mina looked through the peephole, because he heard her soft gasp. The rattle of the chain and the dead bolt had him gritting his teeth. He fought back the urge to throttle the strange man, until Mina opened the door.

She had a pen sticking out of her messy topknot, and she wore those skimpy yoga pants she preferred when she was working from home. Hem slammed the door behind him, dragged Mina against his chest, and crushed his mouth against hers.

She let out a small yelp and struggled for half a second before her fingers dove into his hair and she melted into the kiss. Her soft body against his, her supple lips, and the smell of passionfruit in her hair helped soften some of his edginess.

He stepped back and tugged Mina to his side before facing the other man. "It'll piss Mina off if I'm an asshole to you, so I'm going to try to restrain myself. Mina, who is this guy and why is he in your apartment?"

"Hem!" Mina snapped.

Hem ignored her subtle attempt at extracting herself. The man in her living room had taken his suitcoat off, rolled up his sleeves, and loosened his tie. His socks were striped blue. He looked like a soft pretty boy with too much money.

Which was ironic since Hem most definitely had more money than this fool.

The man looked over at Mina and held his hands up in surrender. "So this is the other reason why you wouldn't marry me," he said.

"Marry?" Hem repeated. Then he remembered the story that Mina had shared with him weeks ago. Some of his anger eased. "You're Virat Aulakh."

"I am, and I'm not here to poach so I'd appreciate it if you'd refrain from hitting me."

Mina finally wrenched herself away from him and nearly backed into the kitchen counter that separated the compact kitchen and living room. "Shouldn't you be with your family, Hem?"

"I was with part of them. I came to get the rest. Virat, I'm going to assume you were working on something strictly business."

She shoved at his shoulder. "Get out! You can't talk to my guests like that."

"No, I'll leave," Virat said. "And yes, it was business. Yours. I'll let Mina explain."

He grabbed his things and slipped into his shoes near the entrance. He looked like he was going to step around Hem and approach Mina for god knows what, but that wasn't going to happen.

"Thanks for the pizza, Mina. And the advice. Hope you and Josette can work things out for next week."

"Virat, you really don't have to go. Ignore Hem."

Virat laughed. "He doesn't look like he's budging. I wish we could meet under better terms, Hem. Good luck."

With one last salute, he slipped out the door and left Hem and Mina in silence.

Silence that didn't last long.

"How dare you come barging into my home, Hem!"

"I didn't barge in. I walked in. What was Virat Aulakh doing in your house?"

"What, not only am I not good enough to be with your family, you think I'm cheating on you, too?"

"No, damn it, that's not what I mean."

"You have no right," Mina said. She stepped forward and jabbed a finger against Hem's chest. It was hard enough to push him back a full step.

"To want you safe? To want you to myself and protect you from other men? I have every right!"

"So you can tell me again how I'm not welcome or wanted?"

That was when he knew how much he'd hurt her with his sharp words. How could he harm this beautiful woman who bought him so much joy? He should be nut-punched for it. "Mina Kohli, I'll never stop wanting you." He reached out, and when she shrugged off his touch, Hem shoved his hands in his pockets. "I pushed my father for answers. You saw that. And then he reacted poorly to you, which only made me angrier. Then the anger was replaced by fear and shock. When he keeled over like that, I didn't know what to do. I've never seen my father weak or vulnerable like that. I panicked, and with you, I—shit, Mina. I'm so, so sorry."

She rubbed her arms. "Why? Why did you say those things to me? Was it because of Lisa?"

"Partly, yeah. I know that you're not the same. I know my feelings for you are so different than my feelings for her were, but I didn't want you to see my family that way, and then chance losing you."

"You were pushing me away all on your own, Hem."

"And I regret it. I—I'm not good at this. All I know is that I'm willing to do whatever it takes to make it right again." He scrubbed his hands over his face, and when he looked back at her, he thought he saw a flicker of acceptance.

"Okay."

"Okay?"

"Yeah. Just . . . don't do that again, Hem. You used my biggest fear of not belonging against me."

"Oh, hiriye." He opened his arms, but she held him off, increasing the space between them.

"No. I forgive you. I do. I can see that you're sorry, but if you treat me like that again, you won't have a second chance."

He smiled, and hope bloomed in his chest. "Noted."

"Good, but we need some space, Hem. If you stay

here, we both know what can happen. Sex is going to cloud things."

"Wait, you're sending me away because we may have sex?" She was still punishing him, he thought. "I never took you for a coward."

Her mouth fell open. "Coward? Who the hell are you calling me a coward?"

"Then why are you sending me away?"

"Neither of us got a lot of sleep last night. We can't have a repeat performance until we get some space from each other. I can meet you in the morning. Like I've said from the beginning, focusing on Bharat's due diligence case is my priority and tonight I'm going to keep my word."

He stepped forward, radiating tension. "First, you are under no obligation to have sex with me. I want to make that clear. Second, sending me away is cowardly because it means you don't believe me. You still think that I meant what I said. It's not true, Mina. You've done nothing but help since you started working on this case! I don't know how else to tell you that."

"I'm not talking about that anymore. I'm talking about sex, which we'll most likely have if you stay. I don't want to be distracted."

"You know, this wasn't about sex until you made it about sex. I wasn't expecting you to let me stay, but now that you're putting up roadblocks . . ." Hem bent forward and charged like a linebacker. He had Mina slung over one shoulder before she could get out the first yelp. When she swore at him, he slapped her lush bottom and enjoyed her yelp, and the moan she tried to bite off and hide from him.

He rushed into the bedroom that was a few short steps down a narrow hallway and tossed her on the bed. She scrambled up on her knees, and he could see the fire in her eyes thanks to the bright lights from the open windows.

"We are not done with this conversation, Hem," Mina said.

"Okay, we'll pick it up in an hour," he said. And ripped his shirt over his head. He needed to touch her, to claim her as his so that she knew he meant every word of his apology, and that even if she tried to dismiss him, he'd never leave her.

When her eyes drifted down his chest to his un-buckled belt, he knew he had her. "Take off your clothes before I tear them off you."

"You bought me these, you jerk," she said. "You tear them, you replace them." She yanked her blouse off and unbuttoned her jeans. It wasn't fast enough for him. He toppled her back against the bed, gripped her waist-band, and pulled. Both jeans and underwear came off in one go.

He needed to taste her, to touch every part of her. He reached for the back of her neck, gripped her hair in one hand, and pulled her up so that he could devour her mouth. Her lips were as angry and rough as his. It was a battle of tongue and teeth as they nipped and sucked at each other until Hem was breathless for more.

"I'm going to fuck you now," he said when he pulled away. He reached down and plunged two fingers inside her, feeling her soft and wet. He pumped in and out until she squealed and an orgasm gripped her body. She arched against him and he almost roared in triumph.

"What do you want?" he said when she gasped for air. "You want to stop what we have here and send me home?"

"Hem," she panted.

He gripped her hips and yanked her to the edge of the bed. As if she knew what he wanted, she lifted her legs up straight up in the air, and he rested her ankles on each of his shoulders.

"Tell me you want me to stop."

"No," she said, still struggling to breathe. She reached up and pinched her nipples, tugging them into tight peaks.

"I'll walk away and go home now."

"Don't you fucking dare!" she shouted. "Take me, Hem."

"You're the only one for me, and no one else will ever compare to you." Without another word, he plunged into her.

She screamed and the echo reverberated in his head. She was so tight, so soft against him, and all he wanted to do was drown in her.

His Mina. His strong, intelligent, beautiful Mina.

He couldn't slow down, couldn't stop himself from fucking hard and fast into her now. Her breasts jiggled, and her hips lifted off the bed with each vicious thrust of body against body. The sound of slapping flesh filled the air, and soon Mina was screaming his name, begging for him to make her come.

Hem leaned forward, bending her in half until her knees touched her breasts, and he felt her clench around his cock. She began to come, and her pussy milked him until his balls tightened and the orgasm shot up his spine. He shoved inside of her one last time and called out her name.

HEM DIDN'T KNOW how long they lay, wrecked and sweaty, wrapped around each other. Their harsh breathing ripped through the air in tandem, and Hem gloried in the sound.

"I feel your cum on my thighs," Mina finally said.

"I'm sorry. I know we talked about losing the condoms last night, but our first time without it should've been better for you."

"It was. It . . . Hem, I need to get up."

Hem hesitated, but when he saw that she'd already withdrawn from him, he slid off of her and let her leave the room. The sound of her footsteps echoed down the hall, and a few minutes later, she returned, beautifully naked and disheveled.

Mina picked up his shirt from the floor and pulled it over her head. The look didn't detract from her beauty at all. If anything she was even more stunning. Outside the bedroom, she was poised and professional, so this mussed look was only for his eyes.

Her hands were soft as they brushed through his hair. "What happened today hurt, but the reason why I needed some space is because I realized how much you mean to me and how much you can hurt me. This is scary fast, Hem. It's frightening."

He knew exactly what she was saying. He was scared out of his mind, too. Nothing in his life had ever felt like this before.

"What if I told you—" His heartbeats were almost painful. He banged a fist against his chest and cleared his throat. "What if I told you that I loved you and time means shit when you've found the right woman? I spent years with someone and still wasn't sure if she was it for me. But with you . . . with you, I knew the minute you crossed your legs in that boardroom."

Her mouth fell open, and she swayed on her feet. Without preamble, she burst into tears.

"Oh, fuck me. Don't do that. Don't cry. I'll do anything you want. I'll go." At that, she started crying harder.

He moved on instinct. After he picked her up and put her on the bed, Hem tucked her against his body and covered her with a blanket. Then he held her close until her sobs softened to gentle hiccups.

"Why is it so hard to hear?" he whispered against her forehead.

"Because I'm so afraid it's not real."

"It's real. Main tuhadi sari zindagi nu pyar karan di udika kara riha hum."

I have been waiting to love you my whole life.

"Main tenu pyaar kardiyaan," she whispered against his collarbone.

I love you.

He shuddered from the force of her words. He hadn't realized how much he'd needed to hear it back, how much it meant for her to feel the same as he felt. It was a beautiful thing.

He never thought he'd ask another woman to be a part of his life again, but with Mina, it felt right. He pressed a hand between her shoulder blades and pulled her impossibly closer.

"Move in with me," he whispered. The request came from the very depths of his soul, from his need to be with her as often as possible. His hope that he could wake up next to her every morning.

"Hem, you don't know what you're asking of me. Asking of *us*."

"I love you."

Mina closed her eyes, and he could see the thick black lashes against her cheek. "I want to," she whispered.

"My place only feels like home when you're there. Move in with me. We'll learn about each other together.

We'll grow together. We've started with months and we'll end with forever."

She ran her fingertip against his cheek and then tilted her mouth up to his. "I'm not sure yet. This case, my mother's firm. Give me time. When it's just you and me, then I'll give you my decision."

"Promise?"

"Absolutely. I want to be with you, Hem. That doesn't change. Even if you are an idiot sometimes."

Hem kissed her, and his world was right again.

Chapter Twenty

———————————————————

MINA ENJOYED THE precious quiet with Hem through the night, but when dawn came, she couldn't hold back the truth. She sat with Hem at her kitchen island with two cups of chai and the paranthas they'd ordered from a private chef. They'd polished off most of their food before Mina shared all the information she'd received through her new contact at the FBI and from Raj's call the day before.

"How sure are you about Raj's intel?" Hem asked.

"One hundred percent. She wouldn't have told me unless she was positive."

"Okay."

"You're not surprised?"

"I'm relieved that we're getting the answers we need. I knew we'd find them eventually, so I was prepared for the worst. I have to tell Ajay and Zail."

Mina nodded. "I have to follow up with the FBI with more paperwork. I'll probably do better if you work here and I leave."

He pressed his knees harder against her thighs. "Or you could stay. We know we work well together. In the afternoon, I'll take you for a walk, and we can try out that Italian place you wanted to go to last time for lunch. Maybe you can think about my moving-in offer some more."

Mina snorted. "You want to play hooky during one of the most critical times in Bharat's due diligence so you can argue with me about the pros of moving in? No dice, counselor."

"A man can dream."

"It's fast," Mina said. She reached out and cradled his face between her hands. Her big, strong man had such a soft heart. She had to be careful with it. "I'm not saying no. I'm just going to delay the discussions. Okay?"

One hand curled around her neck and massaged at the tension and stiffness. She closed her eyes and groaned.

"Thank you," he said.

"For what?"

"For speaking up in that first board meeting. For never holding back and sort of asking me to a club so we could drink whiskey. For coming out with me to Dosa Hutt on our first date, and for the few stolen moments we shared after that. And for calling the FBI and turning in the tape on your uncle. I know that couldn't have been easy."

"It was actually very easy," she said. "And maybe that's why I feel some guilt."

Hem kissed her then, slow and sweet. When he pulled away, Mina reached up to cup his face, scruffy from a day-old beard. "I love you."

"I love you," he replied.

Her phone buzzed on the counter, and *Dad* flashed across the screen. She debated letting it go to voice mail, but she had to continue acting as if everything was normal. With a sigh, she picked up.

"Hi, Daddy."

"Mina. I need to see you today." His voice was the same baritone sound with a slight accent he'd never been able to shake. The only abnormality was his request. He never called her in for a meeting unless it was carefully scheduled in advance.

"Oh. I don't think that's possible. I can always make an appointment with you at the office for Monday morning."

"I won't be there. I no longer work at the firm."

"*What?*"

"We need to meet in New Jersey, away from the house. Other than that restriction, I'm fine with whatever location is convenient for you."

Mina looked up at Hem, and she saw his eyes narrow. He motioned for her to continue.

"Dad, what do you mean you're not working at the firm anymore? What happened? Did Sanjeev do something?"

"I'd like to ask you the same question. I need your availability, Mina. This is important."

Her stomach pitched at the realization that if her father was ousted from the company, Sanjeev was most definitely going to target her next. How could her uncle do that to one of his most loyal and successful friends and employees? Had the news of the merger falling through reached them so quickly? Or was the decision solely based on her argument with Sanjeev in the office?

"Give me a second to check my calendar." She pulled the phone away from her ear and pressed the mute button. "Did you hear?"

"I heard."

"Where should I meet him?"

"You mean where should *we* meet him. Tell your father that we'll go to Montclair if he's worried about discretion. We'll find a location and you can text him the address."

Mina repeated Hem's message into the phone, and confirmed that she was bringing a trusted friend along. Her father agreed he'd be at the meeting point in one hour. He refused to delay it any longer than that. Mina and Hem would barely have enough time to get ready and leave the city, but it sounded too urgent to argue any more.

"This is a problem," she said. "Dad lived for that firm almost as much as Mom did."

"Then we have to find out what happened." Hem

pulled her into his arms and Mina sighed against his chest.

"I still can't help but think I'm letting Mom down," she whispered. "I spent so much of my life focused on trying to avenge her memory, and now, in the eleventh hour, I feel like I'm not doing enough. Sanjeev is going to take down the firm she built and I'm watching it happen."

Hem rubbed a strong hand over her back. "We don't know what's going on, hiriye. Let's start by meeting your father. In the meantime, just know that there is no way your mother isn't proud of who you are. Let that be enough until we figure out the rest."

Mina nodded and tilted her head back for a kiss. It was over too quickly, but they didn't have the time for more.

They had a meeting to go to.

MONTCLAIR WAS BURSTING with people enjoying an early fall Saturday morning. The air smelled clean and fresh, while the trees were starting to turn red and orange. Mina followed Hem into Java Cafe and to the back of the bustling restaurant. As Mina took her seat at a scarred wooden table, she was glad the noise was at a loud enough volume that they didn't have to worry about being overheard.

"Are you sure I should go to Alpine with you again after this is over?" Mina asked once the waitress left with their orders. "I think it's too soon after the last argument."

"I'm sure," Hem said. "I texted my mother that we'd be there when Dad got home. Both of us. Dad will have his private medical staff setting him up in one of the suites, so he may not be coherent, but Mom really wants to see you."

She reached out and squeezed Hem's hand. "It's not just your brother trying to bleed me dry for information, right?"

Hem laughed. "It could be Ajay. Who knows? He's definitely in CEO mode."

"I bet you were gorgeous as a CEO," she said and leaned forward to plant a kiss against his jaw. He wore a fitted white button-down shirt over a pair of dark wash jeans. When he tucked a curl over his ear, the diamond in his lobe sparkled.

"Darling, I *am* a CEO."

She was about to lean in and kiss him again when she spotted a thin, older Indian man in baggy slacks and a beige shirt step through the door. He carried a briefcase with him and had dark smudges under his eyes.

Her father. The same man who fell in love with her mother while she was raising two boys. The same man who helped her build her successful firm and had a daughter with her.

The same man who turned his back on her to take away the business she'd worked so hard to build.

Mina stood as he approached the table. "Hi, Daddy."

"Mina."

Hem stood as well and held out a hand. "Hem Singh. Nice to meet you."

"You're Deepak's son," Mina's father said, taking Hem's hand in a quick shake. "So what Sanjeev was saying is true."

Mina and Hem shared a look.

"What happened?" Mina said. "What did Sanjeev say?"

Her father pointed at Hem. "Do you trust him?"

"Yes, with my life."

He let out a sigh. "First, my discretion about how I'm leaving the company is the one caveat in the severance package. I'd appreciate it that you never mention this conversation. Please, Mina."

The way he said *please* had her pausing. Her father never asked her of anything in such a polite tone. His seriousness had her on edge.

"I'll keep what you say in confidence."

"They're going to fire you."

She'd known what was coming. In the back of her mind, she'd always known it would end, but she never imagined that her father would be a part of her uncle's decision in this way.

And she thought she had more time.

She reached under the table and gripped Hem's hand. His long fingers tangled with hers and kept her grounded, even as the breath exploded from her lungs in a heaving gasp. She tried to muffle the sound, but her whole body felt the blow.

"Mina," her father said quietly.

"No. Tell me what happened."

"Okay ... okay, if you want. Both of your uncles called me into the office late last night. Cheryl from Human Resources was also present. Sanjeev and Kumar received word that the merger between Kohli and Associates and J.J.S. Immigration Law was off and believed that you were the reason behind terminating the lucrative deal."

"No, I believe I was the reason behind that," Hem said.

His soft amusement helped Mina relax. When she was home, alone in her room, or in the shower, she'd unbox her emotions. Right now, she knew there was something more her father had to tell her.

"Sanjeev also mentioned that you'd jeopardized your position as head of the compensation board performing due diligence review at Bharat. That you would be removed from your position as of Monday and another one of his . . . connections would take over and present the findings to both the board and the major shareholders."

"Like fucking hell."

"There is more. Sanjeev then suggested that I make a choice. I either sever all personal relations with you and publicly denounce you as my daughter so I can stay with the firm . . . or as equity partner, I accept a severance package and sell my portion of the company to Sanjeev."

"And you chose to . . . to maintain our relationship?"

A flash of hurt crossed his face before he hid it behind his chai latte. Mina felt a burning in the back of her throat and also drank from her mug to soothe the ache.

"I understand why you could be surprised by that."

"Daddy, how could you do that to Mom?" Mina whispered. "I know I've asked you this before when I first found out after the accident, but I want you to be honest with me. Why did you do it?"

"Because your mother *was* an alcoholic," Hem said quietly.

Mina felt her stomach drop, and she turned to the man she loved. "What did you say?"

Hem's expression showed so much remorse. "Hiriye, I was going to tell you sooner. I know I should've said something, but . . . well, when we did a background check on you, we asked our team to first provide a preliminary report, which they did right away. Then we requested that they probe a little deeper into your history. Your mother was in rehab. More than once. For alcoholism. She showed up to court intoxicated and she was on the verge of losing her license."

"It's true," Mina's father said. For the first time in their lives together, he looked lost. Confused. His hands shook as he pressed his palms flat on the table. "I never knew how to tell you. As the years passed, it became easier for me to hide the details and keep the truth to myself. I wanted you to keep the image you'd preserved of your mother, so I made sure to say that she almost never drank before that night."

"I don't understand. If she was sick—"

"If she was sick, then you'd villainize her because you see the world like she used to. In black and white. She was a good mother to you, and she loved you with all your heart. She had flaws, Mina. Like we all do. And her flaw led to her death. She paid for it, and her memory shouldn't be remembered for that shortcoming alone."

Mina fisted her hands and tried to hold back her anger. If her mother had been sick, then she'd needed help. She'd needed support. Instead, she'd lost everything. To make matters worse, her reputation was ruined.

"How could you let her get that bad?" Mina hissed as she leaned across the table. "You stayed quiet and, what, she got worse? Then Sanjeev and Kumar took advantage of her, and you sided with them. Why, damn it? Why would you do something like that?"

"Because," he said softly. "Because as much as I loved your mother, I resented her, too. We were happy for so long together, and then she started drinking, and it became a chronic condition so quickly. She took away years of happiness from both of us. I spent so much time trying to make sure she didn't look or act drunk in front of you. That's why I used the pretense that she worked such long hours. I then started taking on some of her casework, too. It took me a long time to realize that I was so worried about how she looked that I didn't take care of how she *felt*. I'll live with that mistake for the rest of my life, Mina."

He swallowed hard, then took his glasses off to wipe the lenses with a small cloth he'd tucked in his breast pocket. He briefly glanced at Hem, and showed a flicker of embarrassment before he slid his glasses back onto the bridge of his nose.

"At one point in our marriage, we tried to get help. We went to therapy together. And then I started going alone. I never told you any of this, because you deserved a normal childhood. Neither your mother nor I had one. I was the son of a poor village farmer and I had to work even as a child. Your mother . . . Well, you know her story. An innocent childhood was the one thing I could give you."

"Daddy," Mina whispered, aware that tears were tracing down her cheeks. Hem's arm wrapped around her shoulders and lent her the strength she needed.

"Two weeks before your mother's accident, Sanjeev and Kumar convinced your mother to sign over a percentage of the firm. I wasn't there and didn't even know that it happened. Then, she appeared in front of a judge inebriated and ended up having to appear in front of the New Jersey ethics committee. Your uncles suggested that I tell her to sign over more shares to Sanjeev and myself in equal parts to protect our clients. I scared her, I admit, into believing that she'd lose everything after the ethics case, and she readily agreed to my plan.

"Sanjeev confronted us with the truth of what had

happened the night of her accident. I was horrified, stunned even, that I had played a part in passing your mother's firm into his hands. Meanwhile, your mother simply got up from the boardroom table that night and left. It was the last time I saw her. My only focus since has been work and you, Mina."

Mina closed her eyes and pressed her face in the crook of Hem's arm to hide her tears for a moment. She felt him rub her back, then press a kiss against the top of her head. His hold helped Mina regain her composure, and after another few moments, she sniffled once, twice, and then pulled back.

"Thank you," she finally said to the grief-stricken man across the table. "Thank you for telling me the truth. It means more to me than you know."

"I feel like there is still something missing," Hem said. "Why did Mina's uncles hate their sister so much? Why were they so hell-bent on taking over the company?"

Mina's father sighed and cupped his bony hands around his mug. "That's a very long story, puttar."

"Is there a shorter version you could share?"

"Mina's mother was a strong woman, and she had to raise two boys who were always comfortable bending or breaking the rules. She struggled with them, and often had to give them ultimatums they didn't like. Sanjeev and Kumar developed their own kind of resentment, but it had a longer time to culminate. I will tell you this. Their personalities haven't changed much. The fact that they aren't hustling on the street is a testament to how much your mother did for them, too."

"So my mother wasn't just good to me," Mina said softly. "God, I can't believe I'm about to lose the firm. Now that both of us are out, Sanjeev has all the power over Kohli and Associates and I have none. He'll never give back the legacy that Mom left behind."

"Beta, you're so smart, and you still haven't figured it out yet?" her father asked.

"Figured out what?"

He reached out and grasped her hands. His fingers were cold, and they trembled when they first touched her, but the sensation was comforting. "Mina Kohli, daughter of mine, the firm was never your mother's legacy. *You* are. You are the treasure she left behind."

Mina squeezed his hands, unable to speak as the burning in her throat stopped all words from coming out. She wanted to thank him, to tell him how much that meant to her to know, but all she could do was nod.

"I have something for you," he said. He pulled away from her and took out three worn leather notebooks tied together with red thread from his suitcase.

"What are those?" Hem asked.

"Journals. These include her entries from rehab and where she talks about how much she wants to be a better person. I had weeded these out and hoped that one day I could share this truth with you, too."

Mina took them from his hands. They still smelled

like incense and lavender. The soft edges of the leather binding and worn pages were beautiful reminders of the past. That was when she truly realized how much her father cared for her. He'd done so much to protect her. "This means the world to me."

He let out a shuddering breath. "I thought I was helping when in fact I was making it worse."

Mina had been worried that the barely there relationship with her father would suffer when she confronted Sanjeev, but now she knew she was developing a stronger relationship with him than ever before.

"Thank you, Daddy. This means so much to me."

"You mean so much to me, Mina. I'm sorry I haven't told you that enough."

Mina cleared her throat and put on her brightest smile. She had journals and more information about her parents' past than she could've imagined. Later, she would need time to process it, but for now, what they'd discussed was enough.

"Thank you for telling me about Sanjeev's plan, too. I know that you loved working at Mom's old firm. What are you going to do now? You can retire early if you want."

"No, I'm not ready to stop working. I still have another decade in me at least. I'm thinking about practicing from the house. I can easily convert some of the room downstairs into office space."

"That's a good idea," Hem said. "And frankly, you'll probably have clients from Kohli coming to you after Sanjeev is held accountable for his actions."

The older man's eyes went sharp as he narrowed them on Hem. "What do you mean?"

"He means," Mina said with a deep breath, "I filed an economic espionage and trade secrets violation complaint against Sanjeev yesterday."

The waitress came by the table again. "Is there anything else I can get you?"

"Yes," Mina's father replied. His face was a mask of shock. "We need menus. We're going to be here for a little while longer."

Chapter Twenty-One

MINA SPENT THE rest of the weekend preparing for Monday morning. She knew that she was about to go into her mother's—no, her *uncles'* law office one last time. She was wound up all day Sunday and was still tossing and turning at three in the morning when Hem decided to help her sleep by tiring her out. He pulled her out of bed, pressed against her shoulders until her breasts were flush against the cool glass wall overlooking the city lights, and fucked her from behind. For a blissful period of time, she was completely consumed by him as he gripped her hips with powerful control and slammed into her. The sound of their flesh slapping against each other mingled with her breathy moans and her gasps of pleasure. She came twice before he emptied inside of her, and dawn lightened the sky.

"I'm not done with you yet," he said as he carried her to the bathroom.

She was still basking in the afterglow of pleasure when he soaked with her in the bathtub and used her vibrator that she'd brought from her condo. He sat behind her, rough muscles and thick chest hair against the soft curves of her body. The water was deliciously warm as he gently touched the tip of the sex toy to her clit, bringing her to the edge of ecstasy over and over again, before she thrashed in the water and screamed with release again.

She practically limped to the shower to rinse off and felt deliciously sore in all the right places as she put on her burgundy power suit and matching sky-high heels. A cook left two plates of avocado toast at the breakfast bar before discreetly slipping out of the room.

"I don't think this will take too long," Mina said as she bit into her toast.

Hem was still fixing the diamond cuff links in his French cuff custom fit shirt. "Good. I don't like it that you're going in there at all."

"It was going to happen sooner or later," she said.

"Hiriye, what do you think was the final straw for your uncle?"

Mina shook her head. "I'm not sure. He may have gotten some intel from his mole. Or he figured that I was going to do something after I confronted him in the office, so he wanted to make the first move."

Her phone buzzed and she picked it up to read the text.

> CINDY-PARALEGAL: Hi, I got a strange message from your uncle.
>
> MINA: What was it?
>
> CINDY-PARALEGAL: I was told to file notices to all your clients that you'll be transferring your cases immediately to other members of the law firm.

Mina closed her eyes and felt a pang of hurt in her heart. Hem's hand on her back was warm and reassuring.

> MINA: Cindy, were you supposed to tell me?
>
> CINDY-PARALEGAL: No, I was told that I'd be fired if I warned you.
>
> MINA: Thank you for warning me anyway. Go ahead and do what you're told, but if you could add a line and let the client know they can reach me on my personal cell if they have any questions, I'd be forever grateful. If anyone questions it after the letters are sent out, just say that you always added that information in my previous letters.
>
> CINDY-PARALEGAL: Mina, what's going on????
>
> MINA: I promise I'll explain everything to you later.
>
> CINDY-PARALEGAL: Okay

"What did she say?" Hem asked.

She was about to answer when Mina's phone buzzed again.

> BECCA-ASSISTANT: your uncle just emailed me and told me I had to put your stuff in boxes bc you'll be picking them up today. WTF??!!!???
>
> MINA: If you could also back up the folder labeled Personal on the desktop and put the data on a drive, I'd appreciate it. No other requirements.
>
> BECCA-ASSISTANT: *cry face emoji* You got it. Dammit, Mina, I want to know what's happening!
>
> MINA: I'll tell you soon.

Mina put her phone away and quickly turned to Hem, who wrapped her in his arms.

"I'm so sorry, baby," he said.

She kissed Hem with an edge of desperation and then spent her last twenty minutes in the penthouse reassuring him that she'd be fine on her own. It was going to happen, and she was content with that, even if saying goodbye to the firm was like letting go of a goal she'd always imagined she'd achieve one day.

Mina took an Uber to the office as she prepared for the ax to fall. She stepped out of the car and was in front of the firm's building when she received an email from Sanjeev to go straight to the largest conference room on the floor.

With a deep breath and the clear knowledge that she had the memory of her mother, her father, and her lover with her, she made her last trip into Kohli and Associates.

When she entered through the glass double doors, an audible hush spread across the floor. Heads popped up behind cubicle walls and her coworkers and peers stared openly at her.

Everyone knew.

That killed some of her misery. There was no way she would look like a sad, kicked puppy that was being escorted out of a place that had once been built on dreams and hopes for her future. Mina's chin went up and she strode toward the conference room, waving at gawking faces as she passed.

Sanjeev, Kumar, and Human Resources staff sat at the table when she entered. Sangeeta, Sanjeev's executive assistant, sat at the end of the table, avoiding eye contact.

Mina feigned surprise in the doorway. "I have a lot to do today. What's all this?"

Kumar motioned for her to sit. "This will only take a moment," he said.

She dropped her tote bag on the table and collapsed in one of the chairs, as if she owned the place. "Am I getting my partnership position?"

The Kohli brothers laughed as if she'd told the funniest joke they'd ever heard. When they got their humor under control, Cheryl from HR slid a piece of paper in front of her. "You are being terminated from Kohli and Associates effective immediately."

"*What?*" Mina said. Her tone must have been convincing, because Sanjeev and Kumar turned to each other and smiled.

For the first time, she didn't feel like she was fighting a losing battle. Despite her current predicament, her uncles thought they'd one-upped her, but they didn't realize her father would take her side. She felt another wave of gratitude for her surviving parent.

"Due to a series of missteps on your part as an employee, including your unfortunate relationship with a client's son and your failure to make sound decisions and facilitate a profitable merger, I'm sorry to say we are letting you go," Cheryl continued.

"Seriously? That's the excuse you're going to use after I called you out last week?" Mina saw Sanjeev redden and felt a moment of satisfaction.

"We're trying to do this in a civil fashion, Mina."

"Yeah, I can see that," she said. "Also what proof do you have that I'm in a relationship with a client's son?"

"You don't think I keep an eye on you, little girl?"

"You spied on me?" She knew he had, but the idea still made her skin crawl. Did he know about the countless nights she spent with Hem?

He smirked at her now, as if he was reading her thoughts.

Screw him. Even if he had known about her weekends or after-work dates, Sanjeev didn't understand the most important part of her relationship, and that was how she felt about Hem.

"You're disgusting, old man."

"It was worth it. Now it's time to turn in your key card."

She practically threw her badge at him, for the effect of it all. "You're doing this because you're into something illegal with Bharat and I found out."

Cheryl gasped and Sanjeev slammed a fist against the desk. "Don't even think about spreading those lies!"

"They aren't lies, and you know it."

"Your accusations are empty and meaningless. No one will believe you over me. We all know you've wanted this firm. They'll view your words as a desperate attempt to get it. I wonder what your mother would think of you now? Getting fired from the very business that she started."

There was a stretch of silence, and Sanjeev stared at her, as if expecting her to argue.

She sat relaxed in her chair, with one raised brow. "Say what you want to, Sanjeev."

Cheryl cleared her throat and pushed a piece of paper in front of her. "This is a nondisclosure form. We will not share your termination with other law firms that you choose to work for if you agree not to disclose office information. This is outside of your client files, of course, as that's covered by ethics laws."

Mina glanced at the NDA and laughed. She picked

it up and tore it in half. The stormy expressions on her uncles' faces were priceless. "Tell all of New York that you fired me, and I'll make sure I tell all of New York how you tried to whore me out to acquire an immigration firm. Let's not forget how you stole trade secrets from Bharat, Inc."

"Your career is over," Sanjeev said quietly. "Don't you care?"

Mina stood and looped her shoulder strap over her shoulder. "I don't give a shit," she said in Punjabi. It was the truth, too. She believed her father's words that he'd spoken to her with a thread of steel in his voice. Mina was her mother's legacy. She no longer needed the firm to honor that.

"Cheryl? It's been a pleasure. I'll expect my last check in the mail within two weeks, otherwise I'll start spreading the word that HR here is just as bad as the managing partners."

She turned to go and heard Sangeeta's soft voice from behind her. "I'll walk her out."

The older Indian woman hustled to keep up with Mina's long strides. When they reached the reception desk at the front of the office, Cindy and Becca stood holding file boxes in their hands.

For the first time in days, Mina didn't feel the need to cry. She was content with what had just happened, relieved that it was quick and painless. She felt freed, even. The weightlessness was shocking, and she almost giggled as she took the boxes out of both Cindy's and Becca's hands and stacked them on the floor so she could give them proper hugs.

She turned to Sangeeta who wore an anxious expression on her face.

"Don't let him treat you like shit," Mina said. "You're too good for him."

Sangeeta held out a hand to shake, which Mina found odd, but she accepted the gesture. When she felt the slim cool metal against her palm, her eyes widened.

Oh my god.

Mina palmed the flash drive and then grabbed the boxes. Her former staff called out to text them and that she'd be missed as she slipped into the elevator with a security detail. She absently smiled at them while she tried to think what possibly could be on the drive.

She barely heard the security guard who asked her if she had transportation available to take her home.

"What? No."

"You'll have to arrange it outside. You're not allowed in the building at this time."

"Yeah, I got that," she said.

He followed her through the turnstile and out to the curb. A swarm of employees who were coming in to start their day watched her. She would've been horrified normally to endure such a humiliating experience, but her mind was elsewhere. She needed a computer to find out what Sangeeta had given her.

Her heart swelled with love when she saw Hem

leaning against a town car. His frame was expertly covered in a slate gray suit. The one she'd picked out for him that morning.

The security guard froze, gaping until the driver got out of the front seat and rounded the car to take Mina's boxes from her. Then both guard and driver loaded the boxes into the trunk while Hem helped Mina into the back seat.

She kept the drive fisted in her palm and waited for Hem to join her.

"I'm so sorry, baby. Are you okay?"

"Hem? I'm better than okay." She turned to him and held up the flash drive that Sangeeta had given her. "I think I got the information I need to put Sanjeev away for good."

Chapter Twenty-Two

HEM WAS GOING to hell. He couldn't stop thinking about the way Mina looked so delicious, even though his mother was in the same room. It just felt wrong but he couldn't help it. Mina inspired him in ways that no one else had. He leaned against the kitchen island and watched her from across his parents' great room as she worked cross-legged on the couch with a Macbook in her lap. Her hair was twisted haphazardly on top of her head, secured with a pen, and she still wore the dramatic makeup she'd painstakingly put on that morning, but a pair of reading glasses were now perched on her nose.

The power suit she'd worn to work was brilliant and energetic, but he loved her in leggings and baggy sweaters, too.

"I know Ajay called for us to have a meeting at the

estate instead of at Bharat offices, but I should've taken her home so she'd be more comfortable, Mom."

"Nonsense," his mother whispered. She stood next to him, leaning against his side. "How can I coddle her if she isn't here? Do you think she would like the chai now? I can have the cook bring her a cup."

"I think she needs a little more time. She's busy right now."

When his mother sighed in contentment, Hem wrapped an arm around her shoulder and kissed the top of her head. "Main tuhanu pyaar karda haan, Mom. I love you."

"I love you, too, my serious puttar," she said affectionately. She had to stand on her toes to grab his face in her hands and squeeze his cheeks.

"You happy?" he said when he pulled away.

"Very. She's good for you. You're happy, too. More than I've seen you in years, Hem."

He was going to talk to his mother about the nature of his relationship on Saturday, but after the coffee meeting with Mina's father, he'd decided to go back to the penthouse with Mina so he could be there in case she needed him while she grieved. His love was a vibrant, intelligent woman, but she needed her space sometimes. He looked down at the other woman he loved in his life.

"Mom. I asked Mina to move in with me. She hasn't said yes, but I'm hoping that within a few months, she'll change her mind."

His mother's breath caught, and then she began to sniffle. "You're getting married?"

"No, not yet. The topic hasn't even come up. I know that Mina isn't Lisa, but I still want to give her plenty of time to get used to the idea."

He wasn't prepared, he was never prepared, for when his mother smacked him upside the head and swore at him in Punjabi. "She's a proper Punjabi woman. She's different. Treat her that way."

Hem looked over to see Mina's curious expression. "So by treat her differently, you mean propose right away? Isn't that the same thing I did with Lisa?"

"Don't try to be smart with me, Hem. I will hit you with my rolling pin. Then you'll truly know what pain feels like."

"Okay, can we talk about this after Dad gets better? It's not that big of a deal."

"It's a big deal to my puttar who never loved a woman quite like this before," his mother said, squishing Hem's face between her palms again. "My handsome boy. Go tell your father. A good Punjabi wedding is just the cure he needs."

"We're not—"

"Go!"

With that, he shot Mina one last look, who was still watching him with curiosity, and left the great room. His heart thudded at the idea of marrying Mina. He wanted to spend his life with her. That wasn't even a question. He loved her more than he could ever imagine in such a short amount of time.

But marriage? Mina was already skittish with how fast they were moving. He understood her brain a little bit better now. She liked compartmentalizing, and until Bharat's results meeting was over and a report to the major shareholders was complete, she'd be on edge.

When Mina and he got married—

Hem stumbled on the marble stairs.

When. He'd thought about *when*, not *if*. He'd never had that certainty before. Hem's future didn't seem complete without Mina in it, which meant that . . . damn it, yes, he was going to keep her in his life.

He grinned as he finished ascending the staircase. Maybe his mother had the right idea after all. Hem entered his parents' wing, and at the end of the hall, he turned into the master bedroom. A nurse dressed in simple sky-blue scrubs was rearranging the sitting area while Hem's father sat in a glider by the window. The room smelled like antiseptic and incense.

He called out to his father before he crossed the room. The older man looked a little gray, his hair was limp, and he wore a white kurta pajama with a beige shawl draped over his shoulders.

Hem waited until his father slowly acknowledged his presence, his sharp eyes shining with intelligence and fatigue. "Puttar," he said slowly.

"Should you be sitting up?"

His father said something pithy in Punjabi before switching to English. "Sit up, lie down, your mother is always on my case. I don't need you to harass me, either. It's bad enough that my life is over."

"What? Dad, don't say that."

"It's true. No more whiskey, no more cigars, no more ghee, nothing. What do I have to live for? My company is good as gone, too."

Hem sighed and sat on the floor in front of the chair. He pulled his knees up and wrapped his arms around them. "Well, if you're this feisty, then you must be feeling better."

They sat in silence, listening to the easy movement of the nurse in the background for a while.

"I'm sorry, puttar," his father finally said. "I've made one mistake after another. I should've trusted your instincts that it was too premature to go public. I should've consulted with you and your brothers about Gopal owning company stock."

It was the first time Hem's father had talked about what he'd done since their fight a few days ago. The regret was etched in the age lines marring his face.

"Papa, we don't have to talk about this."

Deepak Singh closed his eyes and rested it against the back of the hair. His chest lifted and dropped. "When I came to America, I never thought we'd have all this, Hem. The money wasn't important to me. The life I built for my children. The respect I earned for my work. That's what I wanted."

"I think Mom would disagree about the money, Dad. She demanded you renovate that kitchen and spent over four hundred thousand dollars."

"I'm glad I could give that to her, but she'd be okay using that galley kitchen in the Flushing apartment, too."

"What are you getting at, Papa?"

"I'm saying that we have money, vineyards, buildings, patents because I pursued respect. Now that we've gone public, I've lost the respect of my peers, and I'm losing my money, too."

"Don't believe that for a second. You haven't lost anyone's respect."

His father's labored breathing slowed. "WTA hasn't just taken away my company, they've taken away my pride. What's even worse than that, they've taken away my oldest son."

Hem felt his heart crack and he reached out to rest a hand on his father's bony knee. "I was never taken from you. If anything, WTA brought us back together."

"But you left."

Hem sighed and slipped into Punjabi. "I left because it was the best thing to do at the time for me and for the company. I wanted something different. Don't you see? If it wasn't for you, I would've never been strong enough to start my own law firm. You're the one who taught me that I could do anything. I know that we fought, and I know that a lot of things were said, but believe me when I tell you, there is nothing that will ever come between us."

He held out his hand, and his father looked at it for

a moment before resting his quivering fingers against Hem's.

"Tell me you understand, Papa."

"Okay," Deepak said. "Maybe it *was* the right decision. I think—I think your brother loves your role more than you ever did."

"Exactly. I never left you. I just made the best move so that the rightful leader could take over. Ajay wanted the company to go public. Now, after all this time, I know it was the right move. His instincts are better than mine."

"He's brash, puttar. He doesn't have your finesse."

"No, but that doesn't mean he's wrong. He does his job differently, but you and I both know he does it better. You have to trust him to make the right decisions for the company."

They sat in silence for a long time. Deepak's chair rocked back and forth and muffled noise from the nurse's quarters echoed softly in the background. Hem let out a breath when he finally felt his father squeeze his fingers.

"I missed you."

Hem's throat constricted at the shaky sound of the old man's voice. He hadn't known how important it was to hear those words until his father said them. "I missed you, too, Papa. We'll get through this. I'm not with the company anymore, but I'm here. And so is Mina."

"I owe her an apology."

"Yes, but right now, get better. Ajay, Zail, and I will protect Bharat."

Those piercing dark brown eyes, the same ones Hem saw whenever he looked in the mirror, stared back at him. "It's such a burden I leave you with."

"It's not. Mina taught me about legacy, and we are the legacy you've created, not the company. And Papa? There is nothing we wouldn't do to protect it for you."

"SO MY UNCLE's assistant downloaded all these emails for me. This one is a message from WTA to my uncle requesting Bharat's classified information. And then this one, is where my uncle shared the preliminary patent documents that should've never left the company's hands. I forwarded all of this to my FBI contact." Mina pointed to the screen and watched as Hem's mother put on a tiny pair of reading glasses and leaned forward.

"That dog," she said in Punjabi. "Is this enough to make sure that Sanjeev goes to jail?"

"I think it's a start. It's up to my contact at the FBI to do the rest." She waited while Hem's mother continued to read through the messages Sangeeta had saved on the drive. Mina had no idea why she was talking about work with Hem's mother. Honestly, it was the only topic she could think of bringing up when the older woman approached her. Mina wasn't exactly the most adept at talking to mothers.

Hem's mother sat back when she finished and reached out and brushed a hand over Mina's hair. "This must be hard for you. Going against your uncle."

Mina shrugged, still trying to process the affectionate gesture. "Uh, not that hard actually. Sanjeev has always been antagonistic towards me."

Was that the right thing to say? Should she have been that honest? Damn it, she wished that Hem would hurry up and come back.

"Hem and Ajay told me a little about your family," Hem's mother said. "You wanted to make sure that your mother's death wasn't in vain. I'm sorry you're no longer at that firm, but I'm sure she's proud of you as the woman you've become, regardless of where you're employed."

"I'm starting to believe that."

Hem's mother picked up the cooling chai from the coffee table and handed it to Mina. She stroked a hand over Mina's head again. "A mother knows. Trust me when I say that if she could see you today, see how you're helping my sons because it's the right thing to do, she'd be bursting with pride."

"Thanks, auntie," Mina said quietly.

"You are Hem's, which means now you are mine. You may not like that after a while."

Mina laughed, and the tightness in her chest eased. If there was one thing she knew about Punjabi mothers, it was that they didn't hold back.

"What's so funny?" Ajay's voice echoed through the room as he approached them, phone in hand, suit coat dangling from his fingers.

"We are having girl talk," Hem's mother said as she

stood to greet her second son. "It's so nice Mina is help-ing you with your father's company. Finally a woman to keep you three idiots in line."

"Love you, too, Mama," Ajay said. He collapsed on the couch next to Mina and dropped his head back against the plush cushions. He looked haggard even though it was only Monday. His face was covered in two-day-old scruff and his hair was disheveled and slightly overgrown. Even his tie was askew.

"Rough morning?"

"You have no idea." He grabbed one of her hands and pressed a loud smacking kiss to her knuckles. "Thank you. Thank you and your friend for the information that you've given us. Zail had to let Sahar go and I don't think he'll ever forgive me for it."

"I'm happy to help. I'm sorry about Sahar, though. I only spoke with her for a few minutes but I liked her. It was a shock when I heard the news."

"She's the least of our problems. We still have to flip the board before WTA comes in and flips it for us. If they do, their first move will be to oust Dad."

Mina put her cup of chai down and picked up her laptop again. She tilted it so that Ajay could see the screen. "I may have some information that could help with that."

Ajay took the computer from her and began scroll-ing through the documents at a rapid pace. One eye-brow jerked and his jaw tightened by the time he got to the end. "Did you talk to Hem about this?"

"I did. And then I sent it to my contact at the Bureau. Hopefully she'll have something for you before the board meeting on Thursday. You were able to reschedule it, right?"

"Yes, we're all set."

"I'm sorry I won't be able to be there. I was let go from Kohli and Associates today."

Mina saw the sympathy on his face. "Hem texted. You're better than all of them. You'll shine brighter on your own."

"I hope so. It's just that I've come so far with Bharat, Inc. It would be nice to see this through, you know?"

Mina turned when she heard heavy footfalls coming down the stairs. Hem's lean form came into view and she smiled back at him. Her heart, she thought. She'd lost her job, but she'd found her heart.

"Already putting her to work?" Hem told Ajay.

"No, but I was about to."

Mina noticed the mischievous sparkle in Ajay's eyes. "What are you talking about?"

"Something you said gave me an idea. I think I've come up with a solution for how you could join us for Thursday's board meeting."

Mina glanced back and forth between the brothers. When both of them started grinning at her, she closed the lid of her laptop. "Okay, you have my attention."

Chapter Twenty-Three

——————————————

HEM WAITED AS the board members were escorted one at a time into the conference room. He and his brothers were positioned at opposite ends of the table. Folders and water bottles were placed in front of every empty chair, and the Polycom unit was set up with a moderator so shareholders could join remotely if they wanted to. Press was also on the line. Someone had leaked that Bharat was having a critical board meeting before the third quarter mark, and WTA was positioning for a takeover.

Ajay nodded at some of the seated men and came to stand by Hem's side. He adjusted his cuff links even as he leaned over to speak in a low tone. "Mina is waiting on her Bureau contact to show up. Tiffany and Rafael have confirmed that our security team is waiting on standby if things get out of hand."

"We have to find out what Sahar leaked, bhai."

Ajay grunted. "I hired a new cyber security team to help Sri. You know Mina's friend Raj? He uses this company apparently. So far, they're paying off."

Hem started to correct Ajay and tell him that Raj was actually Rajneet, but Tiffany appeared by their side. "All of the members have checked in. They should all be seated shortly."

Hem looked at his brother and then across the room at Zail. He took a moment to button his suit coat. "Ready?"

"Always," Ajay said. Zail gave them his go-ahead signal as well.

Along the back wall sat Damany Gordon, Bharat's CFO, as well as the members of the compensation committee. Damany held up a thumb.

"Good morning," Ajay said, loud enough to catch everyone's attention. He took his spot at the front of the boardroom table and clipped the portable mic to his suit for the conference call. "Today's agenda includes our standard financial report, as well as the findings by the compensation committee on whether the offer by WTA is worth accepting. Once we finish our report-out, we'll end the shareholder call and then resume with the board meeting."

"Where is your father? I'd assumed he'd be here for an important meeting like this one," one of the board members commented.

Ajay looked over at Hem, who nodded.

"Deepak Singh is in successful recovery from a heart attack that occurred a few months ago. He will be returning to work within the next two weeks."

Murmurs echoed around the table.

"Is he even fit to run the company?"

"WTA's offer couldn't have come at a better time."

"Maybe he should take an early retirement. He's sixty-four after all. He can only be CEO for one more year anyway, according to corporate bylaws."

The board members didn't hold back their comments, which only had Hem clenching his jaw hard enough for his teeth to grind. He looked over at Sanjeev, who grinned like he'd just won a prize. His large paunch stuck out in front of him, like he'd shoved a beach ball underneath his button-down shirt. The man's face was a picture of smugness and satisfaction.

Good, Hem thought. He had no idea what was coming.

"We'll follow the agenda," Ajay said calmly. "My father will release a memo shortly after this meeting."

Ajay introduced Damany, and their CFO walked through the finance report. It looked grim, which was probably why so many of the board members had smiles on their faces. Hem gripped his phone tight enough for his knuckles to whiten. These men were the reason why his father had suffered so much. He was ready for them to get their due.

His phone buzzed in his hand, and he looked at the readout.

MINA: We're ready when you are.
HEM: Give it another five and then come on in

Damany continued in his easy monotone and wrapped up his presentation. He motioned to his assistant, who was taking notes from a chair along the back wall. She stood, reached across the table, and unmuted the com panel. "I will now take any questions from the shareholders," Damany said.

A voice boomed through the com. "This is Robert Douglass, Douglass with two *s*'s. I'm representing WTA Digital."

Hem looked over at Zail, his posture rigid, his face focused, then at Ajay, who raised a brow, arms crossed over his chest. WTA had officially made its first move. They'd have to look into the rep for WTA the minute they got off the call.

"What can we do for you, Robert?" Ajay said.

"That's Mr. Douglass, actually."

A hush fell over the room.

"Mr. Doug?" Ajay said. "Okay, Doug it is. What can we do for you?"

The com crackled again. "Mr. *Douglass*. We're looking forward to hearing your response to WTA's offer. As a major shareholder, we have the right to demand that certain discussions occur with the shareholders present on the call. Unless, of course, you'd like for us to file a report with the SEC for violating shareholder rights?"

Hem laughed, and every head in the room turned to him. He knew an attorney on a power trip when he heard one. "Hey, Doug, this is Hemdeep Singh, interim legal for Bharat."

"It's Mr. Douglass—"

"And I couldn't give a shit. You can demand all you want, but it's a conflict of interest for you to be a part of the discussions. And since we now don't know if there are other WTA employees on the call, we will be closing the conference line."

"We as shareholders have a right to—"

"No, you don't. And your thinly veiled threats about the SEC don't bother me."

Mr. Douglass began speaking again and Hem crossed to the table, leaned between two of the board members, and shut off the com panel.

"You can't do that!" one of the board members shouted.

"I just did."

"You three are trying to run this company like a circus. If we're ready to vote, I'm all in favor of WTA's acquisition of Bharat. It's time for some real direction."

"Of course you're one of the people to say that," Zail snapped, and Ajay held his hand up, palm flat to stop him from moving forward.

"Let's move on," Ajay said. "Can the compensation committee come and present their findings?"

The three representatives in the room stood, tablets in hand. Their smiling faces put Hem's teeth on edge. But before they could speak, the conference room opened and Mina stepped through in her elegant red pencil skirt and thin heels. Her hair was swept up and she wore black cat-eye frames. She looked beautiful.

"Sorry I'm late," she said cheerfully.

Sanjeev sputtered at the table and stood, his face molten with anger and shock. "You can't be here!" he shouted. "You're no longer head of the compensation committee!"

The board members began whispering and speaking among themselves.

"Sanjeev, didn't you appoint her yourself?" someone commented.

"Yes, but she was fired from the firm on Monday. It's apparent that she's been romantically engaged with one of the Singh brothers. Or all of them, for all I know. She's not an unbiased party anymore. Ajay, I demand that you have her removed from the premises! The rest of the compensation committee is ready to present."

Ajay laughed. "I'm afraid I can't tell Mina to go."

"Why the hell not?"

"Because she works for me. She's representing Bharat as a legal consultant."

"What? That's not—you can't—"

"It is, and he can," Mina said. She went to stand by Hem's side. "I'm assuming the committee's recommendation will be to sell Bharat?"

The three members of Sanjeev's new compensation committee turned to each other, then nodded.

None of the board looked surprised. Some even had smiles on their faces. Hem's excitement grew as he waited for the blow that they'd been working toward.

"The Singhs have decided to dismiss the committee's findings and reject the offer," Mina said. "It's clear that Bharat is worth more than the offer is for. Reports will be mailed to board members upon request. We will be sending WTA a letter of rejection shortly after this meeting."

The room erupted. Chairs were pushed back from the table, and grown men were raising their voices as they demanded Ajay do something.

Hem knew he was grinning like a fool when Mina calmly stuck two fingers in her mouth and let out a piercing whistle that had everyone in the room freeze. She looked up at him with a serene smile on her face.

If Hem didn't love her as much as he did already, he would've been bursting with it then.

"Mina, we have done our due diligence and are as qualified as you, if not more so, to make a decision on behalf of the board," said Connie, one of the more vocal members of the committee. "You have no right to come in here and ignore the work that we've done on your behalf."

"I was fired this past Monday, not a month ago," Mina said. "I've reviewed your reports and put together most of the work myself. Your judgment is compromised because we've found evidence of large lump-sum payments made to you by WTA. Large payments have been traced to the other members of the compensation committee as well."

"You three have to be the biggest idiots ever," Zail said with a laugh. "Every thriller on the planet can tell you not to use your checking account for bribe funds."

Mina walked over to the conference room door and opened it. Two men in black suits appeared at the entrance. "All three of you must follow these nice gentlemen at this time. They have a few questions for you."

Hem studied the shocked faces of the remaining people around the table as the compensation committee was escorted out of the room. He turned back to the doors where Mina stood. He raised an eyebrow, and when Mina winked at him, he knew that she'd been able to get the Bureau to appear at the office in person.

Son of a bitch.

Mina motioned for someone else to enter, and a petite Asian woman walked in, wearing a suit and a riot of tight curls around her face.

"Our guest speaker has arrived," Ajay said cheerfully.

"This meeting is like a Warren Buffett shareholder circus, Ajay," a woman said at the table. "First you hang up on our shareholders, then you're inviting these *people* into the room. What the hell is happening?"

"Through the due diligence process, we've realized that there have been a few employees and board members who have been taking bribes and exchanging trade

THE TAKEOVER EFFECT 2

secrets," Ajay said. "This has led to a staggering effect on sales, which is why Bharat isn't living up to its market potential."

"So we're cleaning house," Hem said. He walked over to stand next to Ajay, and Zail did the same. "This company has been our father's dream since he arrived in this country decades ago. WTA Digital would like to use his genius, and the genius of the employees currently under our protection, and weaponize it. That's not going to happen."

"Sanjeev Kohli?" Mina said. "I believe Josette would like a few words with you. Can you please follow her out of the room?"

"I'll do no such thing!" he shouted. "I'm the one who belongs here, not you."

"Mr. Kohli, this is no longer a request," Josette said.

His face was blotchy with anger. "How dare you speak to me that way!"

Josette motioned for him to get up from the table. "If you'd prefer to do this here, then I'm not opposed to it."

"I'm friends with Deepak. He'd never stand for you treating me like this."

"Our friendship is over."

Hem froze, as did Ajay and Zail. They watched in shock as their father used a cane to enter the room. His assistant hovered behind him.

No one moved for a moment, until Mina spoke. "Get your father a chair. He should sit."

Her words had Zail moving with lightning speed.

He led his father to the front of the room and into the high-back chair that had remained vacant.

"What are you doing here?" Hem asked.

"Didn't think I'd miss this show, did you?"

"Deepak, I'm glad you're here," Sanjeev said. His voice sounded a little calmer, but he remained standing. "Your sons and this—this spawn of my dead sister are trying to have me dismissed."

"Sanjeev, I trusted you with my vision. But now that I've seen your emails, I know now exactly what you're capable of."

"Emails?" Sanjeev's face morphed from confusion to anger. "Mina!"

"I'm really going to have to insist you come with me now, sir." Josette motioned for him again. This time her aggressive stance was unmistakable.

When Sanjeev remained rooted where he stood, Josette motioned for her two guards to come forward. "Mr. Sanjeev Kohli, you are being charged with violating the Economic Espionage Act and with two counts of bribery. Please come with us."

"Here, I'll help, Josette," Hem said before her security detail could assist. He rounded the table and gripped the back of the shorter man's neck. When he squeezed, feeling the give of fat and rolls of wrinkled skin, Sanjeev yelped. Hem easily maneuvered him out of the boardroom, despite his struggling. The whole process took two minutes but made Hem feel infinitely better.

Josette took over when they cleared the doors, and

just like that, Sanjeev was gone. He was most likely going to serve a prison sentence as well as pay a hefty fine.

Hem moved to stand next to Mina, placing a hand on the small of her back. She shuddered under his touch and whispered to him, "It's finally over."

They listened as Ajay redirected the meeting for the rest of the members. "Ladies and gentleman, it has come to our attention that there are a few more of you that have been trading secrets with WTA for profit and to the detriment of Bharat, Inc."

Systematically, they revealed the evidence in the public forum, forcing reactions of surprise and confessions made from desperation. In twenty minutes, four more board members were removed.

And then it was done.

Hem and his brothers, with the help of Mina Kohli, had gotten rid of the snakes for good.

Chapter Twenty-Four

MINA WOKE UP to the soft brush of fingers against her cheek. Hem pushed her hair out of her face to expose her to the bright morning sunlight.

Instead of rolling over and snuggling into him, she pulled one of the pillows out from under her head and covered her face. She lay on her side with Hem snuggled against her, and she could feel that he was already awake.

"It's too early, Hem," she snarled. She loved the man but she was definitely going to kill him if he didn't let her sleep.

Hem's soft chuckle hinted that he was inching closer to her. "We have a lot to do today," he whispered. "Starting with each other."

His hands stroked over her thigh and one of his legs pushed gently between hers. Mina grunted, but she didn't push him away. Her awareness grew when hand snaked over her torso and cupped her mound.

"Are you awake now?" he whispered.

She let out a soft sigh when he pressed slow, firm circles against her clit.

It took less than thirty seconds for his touch to elicit a moan. She shoved the pillow off her face and rolled onto her back. Hem's lips were waiting for her, and she cupped his face when their mouths met.

Their lovemaking was slow and sweet. Hem took his time pleasuring her, and Mina slowly stroked her hands down the ridges of his back. When he finally slipped inside her, she was fully awake and all her thoughts were of Hem. He lifted her to the highest peak of an orgasm, and when she tumbled over, he found his release as well.

What felt like hours later, Hem rolled to his side and pulled her against him.

"I love you," he said in Punjabi.

"I love you," she repeated. "Even though you woke me up when I so desperately wanted to sleep."

"I wish I could let you," Hem said.

"You could've," she said and stretched against him. Even though her body felt loose and limber after her quick mattress workout, she still felt like she could use a few more hours of rest to let her brain catch up. "What time is it anyway?"

"Almost 11:00 a.m."

"Hem, if a person spends the day with the FBI, then

st of the night working with the press on interviews
nd releases, they deserve as much sleep as they want."

Hum nuzzled his nose against hers. "I'd love to give
you that luxury, baby, but I want to take you out somewhere before my parents come for dinner tonight. They
want to celebrate."

"Oh, that's right. What are we celebrating?"

"We're going to toast a successful board meeting,
but I think they just want to spend more time with you.
But don't worry about that right now. Come on. Let's get
ready. I'm going to take you out."

Mina groaned when he got out of bed. He'd been so
warm and snuggly. The blankets weren't so bad, though,
and she tried to cover her face with them, when he
ripped them off the bed.

"Hey!"

"I guess you need some help," he said cheerfully and
carried her into the bathroom.

"I better get coffee!" she shouted as he ushered her
into the shower stall.

An hour and a half later, after Hem spent a little
longer than necessary taking care of her with the help
of strategically aimed body jets, they turned down a side
street in Jersey City.

"I didn't even get coffee yet," Mina mumbled. She
was barefaced and had barely managed to get her hair
pinned up.

"I thought you might want some chai instead."

"Chai?" The thought had her cheering up as He[...]
parallel parked the car in the first available spot. "Where
are we getting chai here? Isn't there a Little India section
a few streets away?"

"You'll see."

He rounded the car and met her on the sidewalk.
They strolled hand in hand toward the closest intersec-
tion. The air was crisp, and the feel of Hem against her
side made her brim with love. It was surreal how quickly
her life had changed in such a short amount of time.
She'd woken up on her thirtieth birthday alone and
with the single focus of honoring her mother's memory.
Now, she was making peace with the past and looking
to build a future with someone new.

Hem pulled her to a stop in front of a store. "Here
we are."

Mina looked up and burst out laughing at the sign.
"Parantha Palace? Really?"

Hem shrugged. "It's supposed to have some of the
best paranthas in the tristate area. The restaurant owner
has a successful place in Delhi and then tried to make
it work in Queens, but they were competing with other
fast food Indian chains like Dosa Hutt. So Jersey City
became their new home. I think it's going to work out
for them."

Mina smiled. "Okay, let's go in."

They stepped through the doors into a charming
café with thick wooden tables and Bollywood post-

s on the walls. The smell of spices filtered through
the kitchen door behind a glass counter. Mina's eyes
nearly fell out of her head when she saw the extensive
menu.

"Why are we here again?" she asked.

"Just order. I'll tell you when we grab a table."

She went with the basics and decided that they
should come back so she could go down the menu in
order and try something new each time. Hem got the
same, and after paying at the counter, he led her to a
table in the back of the restaurant.

"So?" he said. "What do you think of this place?"

"It's cute. What brought this on, though?"

Hem reached across the table, hands up. When she
put her palms against his, he gripped her fingers. "Our
first breakfast together. We had paranthas."

"Our first . . . oh!"

"I thought this was . . . fitting after that night. I
know my family has said it, but I don't think I have yet.
Thank you. Thank you for coming to us, for helping us,
when you didn't have to. I know that going against your
mother's firm wasn't something you ever wanted to do,
but—"

"No," Mina said. "No, stop. Hem, my uncle was
wrong. What he was doing was wrong. And after talking to my father, I know that my mother's firm closed
the day she died."

A waiter brought two steaming-hot cups of chai to
their table, forcing Mina and Hem to pull apart.

"Want to know why I really brought you here?" Hem asked.

"Why?"

"Because I think this could be our Dosa Hutt."

"What? What do you mean?"

He rubbed his chin and then the back of his neck. "Mina, we've only been together for a short period of time, but you're different than . . . well, you're different to me. My parents understood that their relationship would last, too. That's why they talked about the impossible when they sat across from each other at the Dosa Hutt. They knew that if they were together, the impossible was within their grasp.

"That's what I want for us. When we want to talk about our dreams, we can come here, to our version of the Dosa Hutt. I'll believe in you, if you believe in me."

Mina couldn't help herself. She leaned across the table, grabbed Hem's face in her hands, and kissed him. It was quick, considering their current location, but it felt right. "I love you so much, Hemdeep Singh. Yes, of course I'll believe in you. Always. Here, we're on equal ground."

She felt her eyes water under the intensity of the emotions on his face. He gripped her hands in his.

"Are you going to work with me? Build my firm into *our* firm?"

"You really want me to? I mean, I know that I was temporarily working with you so I could be in that boardroom, but I never expected you to make me a permanent member of your team."

"Partner. I want you at my side. I want to work with you, argue with you, and be with you every day."

"Then yes!" Mina laughed. "Yes, of course I'll work with you. As soon as you put me on payroll."

"Done." His grin was infectious, and it was that expression that had Mina taking a leap of faith and accepting the fact that she was about to have more changes in her life.

"Hem? Because I believe in you, and we can believe in the impossible together, I'll finally answer your question. Yes."

"Yes?" His brows knit together. "Yes to what?"

"Yes, I'll move in with you."

Mina had the pleasure of seeing his face morph into shock. Then she was pulled out of her chair and spun in a circle in the middle of a half-empty restaurant in Jersey City. It didn't matter to Mina, though. She was with the love of her life, and her future had never looked brighter than it did in that moment with him.

"How are you holding up, beta?" Hem's mother asked. She'd arrived with Zail and Hem's father an hour earlier. It had taken her only moments to realize something had happened between Hem and Mina. When Hem had told her that they were moving in together, the older woman had teared up and grabbed both of them in fierce hugs. There was only one way to celebrate, she had said. With food.

"I feel good," Mina said as she helped pour a cup of chai for Hem's father. "I think that after Sanjeev was held accountable, I realized how important it was to do what was right for me versus what I thought was right for my mother."

Hem rounded the counter and wrapped an arm around Mina's waist. "I'm sorry about the office raid at Kohli and Associates today. I know they were only seizing computers and documents that connected to your uncles, but that couldn't have felt good."

It hadn't, Mina thought. She'd been so sure she had shed any and all claim over her mother's firm, but when she'd started getting text messages about the issued warrant and the authorities showing up, she'd thought she might burst into tears. She'd had to go to the bathroom and lock herself in so she could catch her breath. Hopefully time would rid her of that knee-jerk reaction.

She reached up and cupped Hem's face for the briefest of touches. "I have a new firm to get my hands on."

"After the way you helped secure three former Kohli and Associates clients before you even signed the HR paperwork? You have carte blanche."

"Three clients?" Zail asked as he snagged a cashew from the snack tray on the table. "That's impressive. Do you think your father has that kind of talent?"

"I don't—wait, why are you asking?"

Zail shrugged. "He's unemployed, right? And he's not exactly ancient. Younger than dad here. He may be considering in-house work. Hem wasn't filling the SVP of legal position at Bharat on a permanent basis, and it's vacant again."

"Wow, I mean, you'd have to ask him but I think that's an incredible offer."

"I like to work with people with integrity and it sounds like your father has it," Deepak Singh said. "I'm sure Ajay will get the ball rolling."

"We're having him over for dinner tomorrow night," Hem added. "We can also talk to him together."

Zail cleared his throat and shot Mina a pointed look.

"What? What is it?"

"Nothing really, it's just that when I look at your current situation, I'm curious about something. You and Hem. You're going to live together."

"And work together," Deepak added.

"And you love each other," Hem's mother said.

"When is the wedding?" they said in unison.

The cup almost slipped from Mina's fingers. "Whose wedding?"

"Yours!" Hem's mother said.

"I'm not getting married," Mina blurted out.

Wedding? That was . . . a lot. And there were so many people looking at her while she processed that word. The idea of spending her life with anyone was a foreign concept to her. She hadn't thought about it with Hem since they'd been so busy.

But she could see it.

They were about to live with each other, and instead of being fearful, she was looking forward to it. The weeks they'd circled each other had been educational for her. She'd learned how easy it was to be with Hem and how much they had in common. She couldn't wait for them to learn more about each other.

She felt Hem's hand press on the small of her back until she turned to look at him. He took her cup from her hands and then sandwiched her palms between his. When their eyes connected, she felt steadier again.

"Mina and I," Hem said in a firm tone, "will let you know when we're ready to get married. You'll hear our answer first, but until then, please don't try to push us."

"It's probably better you hold off anyway," Zail said.

Mina knew that Zail was giving her an out, and she grabbed it with both hands. "Why?"

"Because we have to figure out how we're going to deal with WTA still. Even though we served them with papers, they still own a large percentage of shares. They get a say in the new board members that will be elected to replace the ones we lost."

"Don't worry about that, puttar," Deepak said. "I've come to trust your brother Ajay. He's supposed to attend a fund-raiser tonight, and the WTA attorney who was on the shareholder call will be there. Ajay is going to have a talk with him to see if he can learn about WTA's strategy."

Mina held her hand up to get the Singhs' attention.

"There was a WTA attorney that dialed in? They're moving in on the company that quickly?"

"Yeah, at least that's what it sounded like," Hem said. "He threatened to call the SEC if we didn't allow the shareholders to listen in on discussions about the WTA offer. I hung up on him after saying that it was a conflict of interest."

"What was his name again, Hem?" Zail asked. "Robert Douglass or something, right?"

Mina's heart stopped. "Wait, wait, wait. Did you just say Robert Douglass? With two s's?"

Hem's eyes narrowed. "Yes. With two s's. That's exactly how he introduced himself."

"Oh my god," she said and covered her face with her hands.

"What? What is it?"

"I know a Robert Douglass with two s's, who just happens to be an attorney."

Hem's mouth fell open. "How? Who?"

Mina lifted herself out of the chair and pulled her phone from her pocket. She quickly typed a message.

MINA: Did your husband get a job at WTA?

The response came almost immediately.

RAJ: . . . you found out. I was going to tell you.
MINA: What the hell, Raj??

RAJ: There is so much more going on than that, Mina. I'm so sorry.

MINA: Like what? We just arrested Sanjeev yesterday and filed a suit against WTA. If there is anything that affects either of those things, please let me know.

RAJ: It doesn't. It just affects me. I'm sorry, I have to get ready for this fund-raiser I'm going to tonight. After that I can talk.

MINA: No, you have to give me something to go off of. What's happening? Please tell me it's a coincidence your husband is going after Bharat.

RAJ: Mina . . . it's so complicated.

MINA: I don't see why.

RAJ: Well, let's start with the fact that I'm getting divorced.

The next exciting installment in the
Singh Family Trilogy is
arriving November 2019!

About the Author

Nisha Sharma is the author of the YA rom-com, *My So-Called Bollywood Life*, and *The Takeover Effect*, the first in an adult romance trilogy. She grew up immersed in Bollywood movies, eighties pop-culture, and romance novels, so it comes as no surprise that her work features all three. Her writing has been praised by NPR, *Cosmopolitan*, *Teen Vogue*, Buzzfeed, Hypable, and more.

Movie rights for *My So-Called Bollywood Life* have been optioned by Gurinder Chadha (*Bend it Like Beckham*, *Bride and Prejudice*) and Susan Cartsonis (*Freaky Friday* the Musical, *The Duff*, *Middle School is the Worst*).

Nisha lives in New Jersey with her Alaskan-born husband, her cat Lizzie Bennett, and her dog Nancey Drew.

Discover great authors, exclusive offers, and more at hc.com.